"Kevin P. [illegible] mond, Va., and hero of this sparkling debut, belongs in the front ranks of fiction's hormone-addled, angst-ridden adolescents, from Holden Caulfield to the teenage Harry Potter."

—*Kirkus Reviews* (starred review)

"*Zero Fade* is wise and wise-assed, hilarious and subtle, knowing and searching. We need writers like Chris L. Terry, unafraid to plumb the complexities and absurdities of race and identity with grace and funk." —Adam Mansbach, #1 *New York Times* bestselling author of *Rage is Back* and *Go the F**k to Sleep*

"Chris L. Terry has bestowed Kevin, the hero of *Zero Fade*, with an especially acute case of teenage angst, and the results are sweet, painful, and very recognizable to anyone who has survived the seventh grade. This is a wonderful book."

—Audrey Niffenegger, author of *The Time Traveler's Wife*

"With sharp storytelling sagacity and attention to detail, Mr. Terry speaks to modern society's invisible men: the black, hip-hop kids of Generation X." —J-Zone, author of *Root for the Villain: Rap, Bullsh*t, and a Celebration of Failure*

"Reading Chris L. Terry's *Zero Fade* offered me a glimpse into a cultural experience that isn't mine, but that I could recognize immediately. Vernacular as world. On the surface, it's just language. But this novel isn't surface. The characters speak in rhythms that reveal emotions not identifiable by just words, but I'll name them nonetheless: humor, sadness, confusion, joy, revelation. It's all here in Terry's first novel, a novel that is practically carbonated, how it sparkles and burns."

—Lindsay Hunter, author of *Don't Kiss Me* and *Daddy's*

"In his engaging and laugh-out-loud funny first novel, Chris L. Terry does an excellent job exploring the complex geography of being a black boy in the '90s. At the same time, this book is populated by characters who reflect the universal vicissitudes of being a teenager that we all can relate to. I am hungry for more work from this talented author." —Bryant Terry, author of *Vegan Soul Kitchen* and *The Inspired Vegan*

"This is a great book about a boy navigating his way through what might just turn out to be the most important phase of his life. His adventures with friends, family, girls, bullies, teachers—and his own evolving values—are subtly drawn, poignantly familiar, and hilarious in unexpected ways. Chris L. Terry has created a protagonist who is refreshingly unaffected and impossible to forget."   —Don De Grazia, author of *American Skin*

"Chris L. Terry's fresh, original voice captures Kevin's struggle as he tries to 'grow into himself' and discover his identity in this funny and bittersweet coming-of-age novel."

—Laurie Lawlor, author of *Dead Reckoning*

CHRIS L. TERRY

2013 CS Curbside Splendor Publishing

CURBSIDE SPLENDOR PUBLISHING

Published by Curbside Splendor Publishing, Inc., Chicago, Illinois in 2013.

First Edition
Copyright © 2013 by Chris L. Terry
Library of Congress Control Number: 2013944486

ISBN 978-0-9884804-3-8

Edited by Leonard Vance
Designed by Alban Fischer
Cover art by Ezra Claytan Daniels

Manufactured in the United States of America.

CS

www.curbsidesplendor.com

CHAPTER 1: SATURDAY

1

Kevin

I never like getting haircuts from Mama, but this one was extra bad. By the end, my hair was jacked up and I was on punishment. She cuts hair in the basement, and I have to sit on a rusty old chair while she leans in behind me, pushing her chest out the way and chewing up my head with my father's old clippers.

Pop's been gone ten years, but I remember little things like seeing his 'fro pressing into the headrest of a car while he drove. I wonder if he still has a 'fro. If he left his clippers behind, has he had a haircut since 1984? That 'fro would be the size of Jupiter.

He probably goes to a barber, because guys go to the barber. Even grown men who are still cool, like

Uncle Paul, go to the barber for a trim. Uncle Paul's hair is always rounded just right. The hairline in back dips down in a U, shaped like a perfect smiley face.

Mama pushed between my ears with two fingers. I leaned forward and took my eyes off the mirror because my belly looked like a basketball.

"Can I get a fade next time?" I asked.

Even scrubby David got a fade last summer, with the little bit of hair on top spraying down to nothing on the sides. Mama pulled the clippers away from my neck and stood there until I met her eyes in the mirror. Then she said, "Kevin, I can't do any fades. You know that I go to real college, not barber college."

Just like always, she pursed her lips, dropped her chin, and nodded. But I wasn't gonna stop asking. Then, she moved the clippers in a circle on the top-back of my head and changed the subject. "Why was that Tyrell walking you down the street with his arm around your neck the other day?"

"He was just saying what's up."

"What's up, huh?"

I didn't want to talk about that no more, so I started blinking and blowing out my nose like hair was tickling it. Water rushed through the pipes. Laura was taking her sweet time in the shower upstairs.

Mama wouldn't drop it. "What was David doing right then? Just walking behind y'all? Tyrell say, 'What's up,' to him, too?"

This got me thinking about how Tyrell's arm tasted salty when he had me in a headlock, and how I wasn't walking so much as skipping along to try and keep up. And, I could just see David trailing three steps behind with his stupid, surprised face and triangle hair that he never picks, slowing down when Tyrell did, watching, not doing nothing. Even Mama could tell David was sorry.

"Naw, he ain't talk to David," I answered.

"He *didn't talk* to David?"

Ignored her and her grammar. Don't care if I sound like some "riff-raff." The clippers made a lawnmower noise, and I watched in the mirror while a chunk of hair floated down onto my shoulder. Mama said, "You gotta stand up for yourself more. People gonna think you a punk if you go around letting people walk all over you like that."

Even Mama thinks I'm a punk? This had to stop. "He was just saying, 'What's up!'"

"Humph. *What's up.*"

I always want to get things right. That's why I try to keep quiet and watch the world. I told Mama that once, and she said, "You'd probably watch a truck coming right at you."

A truck? Uh-uh! She didn't get it, and you'd think she would because, as soon as I try to jump in on anything, she's the first person to check me. Mama moved the clippers up behind my ears. Once, she said me and Pop had the same jug handle ears that she didn't have to fold in during a haircut. Mama's eyebrows went down. The bare bulb glinted off her glasses, and I knew she was thinking of Pop. What did she remember about him?

I put my elbows on my thighs even though that creased up my belly and made me look like the Michelin Man. Fine, orange-haired Aisha would never like me with a big gut and a wack cut. I needed a fade with a half moon curling in off the hairline. Or cornrows, like that D'Angelo singer that Laura's always carrying on about. Or something.

Mama paused with the clippers hovering like a bee. I tipped my head forward, figuring she wanted to clean up my neck. But she just stood there, squinting at me in the mirror, then nodded and said slow, "You're going through a awkward time right now, but you'll grow out of it."

I swatted the top of my head, feeling for the bald patch. All this talk about how she had to do the cut, and she would mess it up. I blinked a bunch because hair was sprinkling into my eyes. Then Mama said, "You're kinda pear-shaped with your booty and your belly, then that bird chest," she pointed the clippers at my midsection, "but you'll grow into yourself."

Her voice was whining into my ears along with the clippers, filling my head, making it hot. Oh hell no. My fists clenched, and I saw her jump in surprise in the

mirror when I made my voice deep like Biggie Smalls'
and bellowed, "Eat me. You fat too," even though it
wasn't true. Then, quick-fast, I ducked under her
slap, hit my knee on the furnace, and knocked over
the mirror leaning on it as I busted to the stairs. There
was a crack, and I turned my head and saw pieces
of the top of the mirror sliding down its bottom half,
making a musical, sprinkling sound and glittering
under the lightbulb. Mama hopped away from the
glass with her mouth so round her face looked like
an exclamation point. Then she yelled, "Hell no!"
and jumped over the glass to come after me, still
holding the clippers. The cord popped out the wall,
and the buzzing stopped. My toes were sticky on the
basement stairs. Mama looked hilarious cussing with
her bathrobe puffed out, but I knew I needed to get
upstairs before she turned the clipper cord into a
lasso and caught me. She came up the stairs yelling,
"Where you going?" and I knew I'd be in even more
trouble if I slammed the basement door in her face,
so I booked it the other way in a circle through the
dining room and living room, feeling my stomach
bouncing and bits of hair flying off my shoulders like
gravel in a movie car chase. When I finally got to the
stairs, I saw the basement door slam shut and Mama
standing there with her shoulders heaving, shooting
lasers out her eyes. I hit the stairs three at a time. As
I turned on the landing, she was using one hand to

grab the banister and the other to hold her bathrobe together. I hopped up the last steps, crossed the hall in one jump, slammed my door behind me so hard it kicked up a wind and rustled my poster of Patrick Ewing hitting a jumper, then sat with my butt against the door right as Mama crashed into it and sent me sliding toward my bed. I've got a little room with a big bed, and I planted my foot against one of its legs and slammed myself into the door, closing it right as Mama yelled, "You need to open this door right now! And clean up all that glass! Coulda killed someone!"

Whatever. I ain't about to kill nothing. She stopped, and I heard her breath wheezing. Across the hall, Laura yelled, "Dang!" from the shower. I yelled, "Eat me," just 'cause I'd already done it once. Then, I heard Mama's breath catch, so I yelled, "I mean you, Laura!" Then Mama yelled, "You talk to her, but not me? You cut your own G-D hair!" and there was a bump on the door and a knock on the floor as she threw the clippers. Mama usually doesn't get this worked, so I sat for a minute, listening to her feet going down the stairs slow and imagining if I just stayed in my room forever, blocking the door and going to the bathroom out the window. Outside, a dog barked, and a man barked, "Shut up," at the dog.

I sat there for half an hour with half a haircut, butt-crack itching because I hadn't showered yet, and waited until I heard the kitchen door shut and

Mama's car crunching the gravel behind the carport. Then, I pretended to be a mouse coming out from under a radiator, opened my door a crack, grabbed the clipper cord and pulled it into my room like I was fishing. I unplugged the boombox on my dresser, sat on the corner of my bed, and ran the clippers over my head, feeling the side that Mama had cut to measure my own work. Hair fell to the floor and gathered on the sheets behind me like waves at Virginia Beach.

2

Tyrell is in seventh grade with me and David. He used to be in the same class as Laura, but he got held back twice. He would have been one of the biggest guys at school even if he was the right age, but in those two extra years his shoulders had grown wide as two sixth graders. He has floppy cheeks that make his face look like a mean bulldog, and he has never once paid for his own lunch.

Truth is that, when he had me in a headlock the other day, he wasn't just saying, "What's up." Me and David had been going to watch a *Simpsons* tape when Tyrell slid out from behind a parked van with a Black 'n' Mild in his mouth. The smoke around his head made him look like a devil when he clamped onto me. David skipped back three steps and never came closer, and I don't really blame him. Tyrell's blubbery arm blocked my ear and made it sound like I was underwater, breathing nasty smoke, with him talking from a boat as he dragged me down the sidewalk.

"That wasn't nothin' yesterday, Boy," Tyrell said.

I tried to "Harumph" through my nose, but it was blocked by Tyrell's greasy forearm. My ears popped, and Tyrell jostled me and said, "Nigga, don't blow your nose on me. Nasty nigga."

I panted through my mouth. Tyrell went on, "That wasn't nothin' yesterday, Boy. You can't just be frontin' on a nigga like that and…"

His voice came in and out every sentence as he threw his head back and talked to the sky like the whole world crossed the line at school last Thursday by kicking his bookbag—by mistake.

I was hustling to class with twenty seconds until the bell. Tyrell was to my right with his boys, a crew of dudes who'd got held back so many times that they were bigger than the teachers. He slammed his locker door open and dropped his faded, old, chewing gum-stuck, inkpen-stained, red backpack on the tiles behind him, right in my path. It was too late to move. Instead, I tried to hop over the backpack, but the toe of my shoe hooked into a strap, and I fell on my side with a foot planted in Tyrell's bag.

It was like someone had pulled the plug on the whole hallway. Everyone stopped walking and went, "Ohh."

I twisted onto my butt and looked up at Tyrell, who was tall enough to knock out a ceiling panel with his head. He had his palms up and his mouth hanging open in disbelief. He started talking in a high-pitched, sensitive voice. "Nigga, you stepped on my bookbag."

As soon as he said, "bookbag," his boys came to life, moaning, "Mmm," shaking their heads and looking down at my feet and Tyrell's backpack. This guy Spayne sucked his teeth and patted his hair, which was more frizz than cornrows.

I tried to pull back my foot, but it was still looped through the strap, and I wound up dragging it toward me. The further the bag slid from Tyrell, the wider his eyes got. I shook my foot free and said, "You dropped it in my way."

"Naw," Tyrell said, settling onto his heels, "You was in *my* way. And you," he bent slow and picked up the bag, showing a dusty, tan footprint next to the zipper, "messed up my bookbag."

Tyrell turned to his friends, as if he couldn't stand seeing the damage. Their eyes clicked from him to me. I stood up and brushed off my butt. I felt stupid as hell for falling over at school.

Spayne put a hand on Tyrell's shoulder and shook his head like they were watching a casket go into a grave. They all hissed steam, "Psssh."

I pointed at the backpack and said, "Where's the

mess? All I see is mess."

Their eyebrows flew up. I slowed down and said, "I know I didn't do all that."

"Oh damn!" yelled someone behind me.

Leo, a hippo with nickel-sized nostrils and a bald head, shook Tyrell's upper arm and said, "Yo, T., he said your bookbag *messed up.*"

Leo couldn't believe that someone would think a five-year-old, once-red backpack, that smelled like it got kept in a fish tank full of old milk, was messed up.

Tyrell shook his head and said, "Nigga, you can't do that."

The bell rang. No one moved from their lockers.

"You got to get me a new one," Tyrell said, nodding.

Leo and Spayne both said, "Yeah."

I hated how my voice was squeaky when I said, "I ain't gettin' you a new bookbag."

Tyrell shook the backpack and said, "Well you ruined this one."

Short Mr. Adams, the history teacher, stepped out of his classroom and started clapping rhythmically, drawling, "C'mon everybody. Get to class. I don't feel like writing any detentions today."

The hallway came back to life, but Tyrell stood still, staring down at me until Mr. Adams walked up from behind saying, "C'mon, Tyrell. Get to class."

Tyrell made a show of brushing off the backpack, then threw it onto his arm and shook his head, sighing out of his nose, before walking past me and checking my shoulder while his boys snickered. I hate those laughs that people do when they're trying to start something. Loud laughs so everyone will look and there'll be a fight. That's what all of Tyrell's boys are. Loud laughs when ain't nothing funny.

That afternoon, while the bus was bouncing down Brook Rd., Tyrell crept up behind me, swung his bookbag into my ear, and said, "You messed it up," like I was a dog that'd just peed the rug.

The whole bus laughed, even gossipy Janelle with the Toni Braxton pixie cut, and I had to duck below the back of the dark green seat in front of me until the stinging tears left my eyes.

The next day was when Tyrell caught us on the block. A couple minutes after the headlock, I was on David's couch wiping Tyrell's sweat off my mouth with a paper towel and feeling pretty salty. David walked out the bathroom like nothing had happened, so I said, "You coulda helped me out there, you know."

David frowned, pretending to be confused, but I mean-mugged him until he went, "I was waiting for him to throw the first punch."

"He had me in a headlock. That counts as a punch."

"But he was just holding you," David said, taking a seat on the other end of the couch.

"Holding me? I ain't a baby."

All that over a busted old backpack. My feet had probably cleaned it off.

3

I got sick of sitting on my bed, scratching hair off myself, so I headed to David's to have a little fun before I got put on punishment. As soon as I got out in the fresh air, my whole body felt stale. My armpits were wet, and hairs were crawling across my neck.

I was still wound up, and the gravel I threw at David's window made a cracking sound like thunder when the lightning's close. David's face appeared, lips curled, and he threw a thumb over his shoulder and disappeared. It's funny when he gets worked up and moves fast. It happens a lot. We met on the concrete porch, and David started in as the door swung open.

"Man, don't be breakin'—"

"But your buzzer busted, and you ain't heard when I knock 'cause you got the TV goin'," I said.

"Ahh, come on up."

He turned back up the staircase, holding the banister and swiveling his hips to reach each stair, booty wagging like a toddler. I caught up and punched him in the rear for giving me lip. A dork like David should be glad I was coming by.

David hopped with the punch and said, "Don't play, man."

His voice hadn't changed. Even Laura's was deeper than his.

"Don't snap my undies."

We both laughed at my *Simpsons* joke.

"You got a tape of last week's show, D.?"

"Yeah, we watched it on Thursday, Kevin."

"Let's watch it again."

The Gunderson's living room always smells like cigarettes and baby powder, and in the afternoon, the sun shows the worn spots on the leather couch in the middle of the floor. Keyboard music was playing on the jumbo TV, where a guy with a Jheri curl and tight jeans ran through a rainy alley, holding a gun. We sat on the couch, and I dug my shoulders into the cushion. I could feel hairs drying under my shirt. David squinted at me and asked, "Why you got hair on you?"

"'cause I got a haircut."

"You didn't shower?"

"No."

I arched my back to lift my butt off the couch cushion.

"Don't get that on my mama's couch!"

He lunged at me with his arms out and shoved me against the couch arm. When I pushed him back, my finger poked into his mouth and slid across his slimy teeth.

"Dang. Watch your nasty mouth."

I pushed him off, and he rolled to the floor with an "Oof."

"Jumping on me like a faggot."

David hopped back onto his side of the couch and said, "Well, if I'm a faggot, then you one too for wanting to hang out with me."

"See, you just admitted that you gay."

Being gay is the worst thing possible. Being gay is fighting bad, sucking at sports, not getting girls, wearing hand-me-downs from forever ago, doing good in class, and looking at other dudes in the locker room. I won't lie, except for doing good in class, I've done all those things. They're easy for a guy to do, but only the gay ones really let it happen.

David waved his left hand.

"Careful with this couch. You know how she is about her couch. She gonna kill me."

"She won't notice. I'll sit still."

I wanted to stay over there forever and not get put on punishment, but I wished I'd showered. The loose hair felt like it was growing roots in my body, and my feet were clammy in yesterday's socks. The man on TV got shot, and he grimaced with his hand over his arm, blood dripping between his fingers. It went to a commercial. I imagined Mama at home, turning in a circle in the hall upstairs, looking to ground me. Nothing happened at home but Mama on my back and Laura leaving to kick it with her high school friends. Not much happened at David's place either, but at least I was doing my own thing. I looked around the room, wishing fun would just appear.

"Can I get some soda?" I asked.

David always had a couple two-liters in the fridge. Cable and soda, David had it made.

"We outta soda."

David narrowed his eyes.

"Some water?" I asked.

"OK, OK, but you gotta wash the glass."

I walked into the kitchen with David, who scooted around to my left with his hands out like a basketball guard, blocking me from the cookie cabinet.

David dropped some ice into a plastic, radio station cup and filled it from the sink. When the faucet stopped, a thin, zipping noise started coming through the window from the alley, a floor down. I knew that noise, but it was out of place. David held onto the cup, and we stepped over to the wide-open window.

All three hundred pounds of Tyrell stood right under us, with wadded up tissue in his nose and a baggy, green t-shirt pulled up on top of his belly. He was pissing on the garbage cans, going so hard the urine roared like drums. Next I knew, David had stuck his arm out the window and poured the water.

Tyrell looked up as the water fell, the puddle growing wider in the air. Even from above, he was huge. You could probably see him from space, like the Great Wall of China. A piece of ice zeroed in on his face. He opened his mouth, and the ice cube bounced off his forehead, then the slap of water, which made the tissue in his nose into a dead flower. Me and David started laughing so I hard I thought we'd bounce out the window next.

The cube skidded to a stop in the gravel. Tyrell wheeled back, blinking and yelling, "Ow!" then taking his hand off his still-pissing privates. He bent down to get his balance, saw the stream of whiz darkening his jeans, and howled like a hound. I slapped David on the back. Maybe he wasn't so sorry after all. Tyrell's shirt fell over his belly. He looked up at me, and the laughing caught in my throat. Tyrell shook his head, drops of water whipped off of his jowls, and he pointed up at the window, yelling, "I oughta beat your ass. And I'm gonna, next I see you out the house."

David was still laughing and thumping the windowsill with his fist. Tyrell blew the wet tissue out his nose, and I realized I wouldn't always be safe in David's apartment. Maybe being grounded wouldn't be so bad. David was pointing into the alley with the empty cup in one hand and clapping my back with the other, hitting a fresh zit that had appeared that morning.

Tyrell used his shirt to wipe water from his eyes, and David said "Boo-hoo" and laughed harder, bopping on the balls of his feet. I pulled him away from the window right as gravel clattered off the shingles and glass, following Tyrell's cursing, "Bitch-ass nigga," through the window. I remembered how I felt two textbooks clapping into each other inside Tyrell's bookbag when he smacked me with it and worried about what a real ass-whooping would feel like. Then, I looked at David, who had sat down at the kitchen table and was still smiling crazy with that cup in his hand, and I just got mad that Tyrell the Bully was throwing rocks into my best friend's apartment. We couldn't even chill inside without Tyrell trying to play us. I grabbed the cup, crouched low, and charged across the floor like a soldier in a war movie. Curse words rained in.

David was getting weak laughing at me squatting on the floor, trying to reach the faucet while Tyrell's shouts got hoarse and started sounding less and less like words and more like, "Arrrgh garba garba garba."

By the time I got more water in the cup and crept back up on the window, the yelling had stopped, and Tyrell was gone. Probably to his apartment a block over, but it looked like he had melted because there was a dark puddle where he had been standing.

A breeze blew a bit of dead grass in the middle of the alley, and an ice cube slid off a garbage can into the dirt. Things were peaceful for the time being. I looked at the water, tipping back and forth in the cup, and remembered that I hadn't put anything in my stomach since before my haircut, hours ago. But the water reminded me of the wet tissue in Tyrell's nose and how I'd have to duck him for at least a week, and I couldn't drink. I poured it out onto the garbage can, and it washed away the piss stain.

We were a few minutes into the *Simpsons* tape when David turned to me said, "Yo, Kevin," then shook his head around all crazy, going, "Arrrgh garba garba garba." We both laughed and didn't nothing else matter for the time being.

4

When I got home, the kitchen was alive. Laura had the little radio cranking, and I smelled macaroni boiling. She was at the stove in the red apron with white hearts that Uncle Paul got Mama for Valentine's Day. It looked like a superhero cape on her skinny body. Super Sister. She stirred the macaroni with a spatula until water splashed out the pot and crackled on the burner. I leaned on the fridge and asked, "Can I have some?"

Laura kept her eyes on the stove and said, "Not

done yet."

"When it's done."

She kept stirring the macaroni. The little ponytail on top of her head moved in a circle.

"You ain't even ask what I'm cooking."

"It's macaroni."

"You don't know that. Could be a bunch of dog mess on it."

I stepped over to the stove, and the steam made my greasy face sweat.

"Don't look like dog mess."

"Boy, what is that on your face?"

"Hair."

I ran my palm across my forehead, then got out two bowls. I tried to snatch a slice of hot dog off the counter, but Laura slapped my knuckles with the spatula, and a hot piece of macaroni stuck to my forearm.

"Dang!" I yelled.

I ran my arm under the sink.

Laura asked, "Why you got hair on your face?"

"'Cause I'm a man."

"Shut up, boy. You ain't shower?"

I really needed to shower. I sat at the table hoping she couldn't smell me.

"No. Mama was being a pain."

Laura grinned at the macaroni. She knew a thing or two about Mama being a pain. I kept talking.

"Tried to tell me I was fat, so I broke out of there."

Laura strained the macaroni in the sink, then turned around. Steam rose behind her and clouded the kitchen window. She was being nice, and she didn't have any makeup on. I was glad she was in a good mood.

"Didn't finish the haircut either, huh?" she asked.

"Kinda did."

"Kinda didn't, too. Look like some of those curls are climbing your head."

She pointed at me and laughed with her nose scrunched up.

I said, "Shut up," covering the back of my head with my hand.

"Shut up don't feed you," Laura turned back to the stove.

"Aight. My bad."

5

It was Redman on the boombox, me on my bed, all the papers and tape cases on my floor, then Mama in the doorway, holding a crinkly black bag from the beauty supply. Her being there made the room feel extra messy. She was saying, "I ain't fat, but Lord knows, I don't have time to not keep on a little weight, what with work, and class, and looking after you and Laura..."

I looked down at my own stomach and wanted to

tell her I didn't really think she was fat. And I wanted to ask how to get rid of my belly.

"... And you're grounded for a week for using that language at me."

But then she dropped the bomb and grounded me, and I just got mad and know what? I admit, I started crying. I hung my head so Redman couldn't see me from the tape player, and tears fell onto the stomach of my shirt, making the blue almost black.

Mama said, "But hey, that's just a week," like she actually felt bad. Then, I felt like even more of a punk for crying. It just wasn't right that she could say what she wanted, but if I had something to say back, I had to keep it to myself, because her life is so hard. Since when is mine easy?

"But I was just standing up for myself like you told me to. You were crackin' on me."

She shook her head and said, "But there's a difference between standing up for yourself and jumping all over people."

She squinted, "You still got hair on you? Best shower before dinner."

Then she turned and stopped in the door to say, "Oh, and before you shower, sweep up the mirror you broke before it turns into even more years' bad luck."

Then she went next door to her bedroom, leaving me to try and figure out that nonsense about jumping all over people. Now there was no way I was asking for help with my hair, but maybe I could give it another go with the clippers after school.

No matter how hard I beat the bed, it was impossible to get all the hair off the sheets. Every morning that week I found prickly curls sticking to me in the shower. Reminders of my punishment. That's what this week was, a bunch of prickly things sticking into me.

6

Mama was at a thing at the church where she works, so I headed downstairs to watch some TV. At least I could do that when I was grounded. Halfway down the stairs, the meatloaf smell got taken over by a chemical burn that fried my nose hairs. Skinny Laura took up the whole couch, feet on the coffee table and hands on her knees, fingers spread like she was holding a basketball. Shiny, bubblegum-colored polish was drying on her nails. She's got far-apart eyes like me and Mama, and with the way her toes and hands were spread, she looked like a flying frog.

"Your turn to do the dishes, Kevin," she said.

While she talked, she stared at a pickup truck going up a mountain on TV while a white guy sang something bluesy.

I stopped at the foot of the stairs. Wasn't much of

anywhere for me to go in the living room.

"It was your turn this morning," I said.

"Yeah, and I did 'em."

"There were plates in the sink when I cleared the table. I even rinsed them for you."

Laura finally looked away from the car commercial and right into my eye.

"Yeah, from when I made you lunch, nigga. So do them damn dishes."

The Laura that made macaroni was Super Sister—the Laura I liked. Super Sister made jokes about Mama and told Tyrell to "Go on." This flying frog on the couch was Saturday Night Laura, a new sister who had started to show up once she started high school. Saturday Night Laura turned away when she was on the phone, ditched me at the mall to talk to the high school kids who smoked near the food court, and said "nigga" when Mama wasn't around. Saturday Night Laura even walked different, with a little bop like she was humming to herself. Her lips were always pursed up, and her eyes were set to roll. Wasn't nothing I could do but go into the kitchen.

But I was mad, and my mind turned dark as the windows. I squeezed extra soap into the sink for more bubbles. A yellow plastic bowl popped up to the top of the water. From Laura's lunch. My bowl had been red. Fair was fair, and this wasn't fair. First I got insulted, then I got a jacked up haircut, then I had to eat wack-ass meatloaf with ground turkey instead of beef because the doctor told Mama we all had high cholesterol, and now the dishes?

The bowl rocked on top of the dishwater and I slapped it so it spun through the air like a flying saucer. That made me smile, and my reflection in the dark window was shadowy, so there were big, dark, zombie rings around my eyes. I made my hands into movie monster claws and plunged them into the dishes.

Something bumped my finger. Then it felt hot. Then it stung from the soap. I pulled my hand out of the water, and a couple pans clanked. Blood and dishwater ran down my pointer finger. The blood scared the hell out of me, and I tried to cuss, but groaned, "Uhhh!" instead. I must have hit a knife under the soap bubbles.

"What was that, Kevin?"

"IIIII...dang."

"Dang, what?" Laura said, stomping into the kitchen on her heels, toes pointed up to save her nail polish.

"Dang, I cut my dang finger."

I held up the finger, and bubbly, bloody water dripped onto the orange kitchen tiles. Laura cut the sink off and got a closer look at my finger. I inched it at her, and she jumped a mile and shouted, "Get your damn AIDS finger away from me, boy."

She slipped in the water on the floor and fell backwards, bony booty first, feet in the air, bubblegum pink fingernails almost touching bubblegum pink toenails. She landed, "Uh!" with her back against the olive refrigerator, and I shouted, "I ain't got AIDS," then started laughing at my sister on the floor.

She slid her foot away from the blood dripping off my hand. Then her face melted from angry to funny, and she laughed, too. She hadn't messed up her nails.

7
Paul

After Paul's fifth gin and tonic of the night, he began to sense a buzzing around him, like an old, neon light. He looked up to see that Winnie's Grill had got crowded with men, a knot of whom stood behind Paul, swaying in unison and singing along with the hopeful piano of Mary J. Blige's "Real Love" playing on the house stereo. Paul pressed forward in his cushion-backed stool so that his head hung over the bar. That's when he saw the red velvet cake—white frosting glowing like a winter moon in its glass-topped dish—tucked onto the shelf under the register since it was after one a.m. and the kitchen had been closed for over three hours.

Winnie herself, pretty and ageless, but with a face hard enough to break rocks, saw Paul staring at the cake. She strutted toward him, fingers pinched into three dirty highball glasses.

"Finally see something you like, honey?" she asked.

Paul jerked his head up and scanned the room behind him by looking in the swatch of bar mirror that wasn't covered with brittle dollar bills and Polaroids of posing regulars, himself included. He cocked an eyebrow at Winnie. She pointed at the cake. Paul smiled and played along.

"Yeah baby, I'm ready to take that home with me," he replied.

He licked his top lip and began working his head side-to-side, locking into the quarter cake with his wide-set eyes.

"You know what? Josephine gonna fix a fresh one tomorrow. Why don't you take that red velvet with you?"

While Paul was picturing a milk chocolate man with wiry muscles unbuttoning a cherry red velvet shirt, Winnie stooped, lifted the dish to the counter behind the bar, and used a square napkin to slide the cake onto a plate, which she deposited in front of Paul.

"Here you go."

"Thank you," Paul murmured, and fingered the wad of cash in his pants pocket, wondering if he should tip. *I'll get her extra on my next drink,* he decided, and sat back in his chair, smelling the citrus of CK-One cologne on one of the divas standing behind him. "Real Love" had ended, and one of them said, "Bitch, it's 'I'm *searchin'* for a real love,' not 'RE-searchin' for a real love.' You ain't in school!"

Paul sat with the cake in front of him, nursing another gin until last call caused a crush of bodies at the bar, ordering final beers and colorful liquor drinks. Three fingers swatted his chest, in the taut spot between armpit and nipple, and a playful voice said, "You didn't tell me it was your birthday, Paul."

He looked up from his drink to see Xavier, a younger cutie with chubby cheeks and bleached orange hair, smiling down at him with his lips pursed.

"You twenty-one yet?" Xavier asked, then leaned back and giggled. Paul cracked a sheepish smile. Barely old enough to rent a car, and he already felt like the old man at the party.

Winnie walked past, deposited a sweating glass of blue booze on the bar in front of Xavier, and said, "It's five for the Alize, honey," before turning away to point at a man who was breathing fast through his mouth and waving a limp twenty dollar bill with a look of panic in his eyes.

Xavier fumbled for the back pocket of his jeans and Paul asked, "Just one drink?"

"I had a couple earlier, too."

Xavier pulled out a shiny, red leather wallet.

"You ain't buying no-one else drinks?"

"Mmm-mmm," Xavier replied, and lowered his head, casting his eyes up to meet Paul's.

"Put that wallet up. I got you," Paul said, and leaned back to reach into his pocket and fish out his roll, which had become damp from being stuck to his thigh all night.

Xavier turned his head, still looking at Paul, then said, "Thanks for the drink."

He reached his hand up and flicked two fingernails along the hairline on Paul's neck. Xavier's touch wiggled through Paul.

"Looking a little wooly there. Why don't you come see me at the shop sometime soon?"

"That'd be nice," Paul replied.

Paul wondered what his ordinary barber would think if he showed up two weeks late with a new cut, then was glad that was all he had to worry about.

"Yes it would. Enjoy your cake," Xavier turned to step away from the bar just as the desperate man with the twenty-dollar bill lunged back, holding four red-labeled bottles of beer, and accidentally shoulder-checked Xavier, who jerked forward, face flared with surprise.

A wave of blue liquor crested the lip of Xavier's glass and splashed onto the front of Paul's leather jacket. Xavier's mouth formed a perfect letter O, dangling under his fussy little mustache. The man with the beers stopped, rocked back and forth on his feet, and frowned down the necks of his bottles. Paul grabbed the bottom hem of his own jacket and pulled it out to pool the spilled liquor and protect his jeans. Xavier set the rest of his drink on the bar, turned to the drunk man with his pointer finger up, and said, "Excuse you."

"Oh, arright. Thanks," the drunk man slurred, then lifted his four drinks in cheers and staggered to his left as if pulled offstage by a vaudeville cane.

Paul chuckled. He didn't give a damn. The liquor would wipe right off his leather, and Xavier was cute when he got huffy. Paul liked a little salt in 'em. Xavier glared daggers at the drunk man's back, then the malice on his face melted into concern as he plucked a handful of napkins off the bar and turned to Paul, dabbing at his coat like a mother might clean her child's skinned knee.

"Look what he did to your jacket," Xavier tutted.

Paul said, "No big deal" and started to brush Xavier's hand away, then realized that he wanted those hands on him, and said, "Thank you. I'll clean it more when I get home. Your drink alright?"

Paul pointed at the bar, and Xavier dismissed his drink with a wave, tossed the crumpled napkins onto the bar, and said, "The drink's fine. I'm driving anyway."

Both men laughed.

"I see you already got something sweet for tonight."

Xavier pointed to the cake, still on the bar in front of Paul.

"Yeah. Winnie gave me that. Caught me staring at it."

"If only it was always that easy."

Paul and Xavier laughed again, watching each other against the backdrop of men hoisting green bottles or taking first sips through thin, black straws. Then Xavier reached for the bar. Paul figured he was grabbing his drink, but Xavier only had one finger out, which he sent over the cake and drew toward himself, collecting a mound of white frosting. Looking into Paul's eyes, he puckered his lips, and the frosting disappeared into his mouth. Then, he picked up his drink and walked off, saying, "See you soon," and leaving behind the smell of tropical hair product.

Paul had wanted Xavier since he'd started coming around Winnie's two-three years ago, underage and in thrall to Panky—a corny, middle-aged saxophonist whose patient, "Let me tell it to you like it is," rap comforted lost, young, gay boys all the way back to his apartment over a Church Hill corner store.

Minutes later, driving one mile under the speed limit on the Lee Bridge with a Hardee's takeout bag heating his lap, Paul moved his eyes from the rearview to the plate of red velvet cake in the passenger seat.

The bridge's sodium lights blued the cake frosting, and he thought about how he should feel bad that the cake was the only thing he'd brought home from the bar in the last two months. But this didn't feel like a consolation prize. It felt like a start. A step in the right direction.

CHAPTER 2: SUNDAY

1

Paul

Sun dried the floor plant, the only thing alive in the apartment besides the man on the bed in back. Paul went from being proud of himself for sleeping through the church bells to angry at being awake. His right hand shot out and grabbed the ringing phone from the nightstand.

"MMM," he told the mouthpiece.

"Paul?" It was his half-sister, Sheila, ten years older than him.

"Mmm-hmmm," he said, the H noise knocking phlegm loose in the back of his throat. The leftover gin in his mouth tasted like the museum's pine floor cleaner.

"Did I wake you?" Amusement tinkled into

Sheila's voice.

For a second, Paul flashed mad at getting woken up, then sat up in bed and let out a noise like a steam engine coming to a stop. The room was dim. Outside, the spring Sunday was alive. He formed his first two words of the day.

"Yes, bitch."

Sheila and Paul laughed into their phones, and Paul smelled his funky morning breath weaving through the receiver's plastic holes.

"You got plans today, baby brother?"

"I was trying to sleep."

The bells across the alley ended with a drawn-out *thonggg*. Paul realized he'd been hunching both shoulders and let them down.

"Well look, I think Kevin needs some time with his uncle."

Used to be that when Paul thought of Kevin and Laura, he saw them as toddlers in green or pink corduroy overalls, faces pretzeled up and crying, giving him spitty hugs, or swiping the pork-specked greens off their plates. That had changed last week when he was over there for dinner and, in an offhand way, Kevin had said, "Paul's like Pop. In the fourth seat at the table."

It had come up because Paul had made Kevin split the rest of the spaghetti with him, but still, it made Paul see something new. It had been ten years since overalls, and Sheila's kids were making their own worlds.

"Uncle time, huh?" he replied.

"Yeah. There's something he might talk to you about, that he wouldn't let me in on."

"Mmm-hmm. He up?"

"You up?"

"Not really."

"Well, come by when you can. I grounded him yesterday, so he ain't goin' nowhere."

"Uh-ohhh. Alright then. I'll be by in a bit."

"Thank you."

Sheila sang the end of "you" with a high note like their mama used to do, then hung up. She called on Paul like this for Kevin from time to time. Kevin, who was navigating the treacherous start of his teen years without a man in the house. Kevin, who might never know that he got his bearish silences from his father, Tarvon. Paul had never thought that he'd be a father figure, but it was nice, and not too difficult, especially since the competition had cut out of town ten years ago, leaving five months of bills on the dining room table fanned out like a hand waving goodbye. And what would Tarvon think about Paul, the man he used to call, "Fairy," being so involved in his family? The thought pleased Paul, and that little bit of spite made him love Sheila's kids even more.

Paul stretched over to hang up his phone. His

shoulders were stiff from his drunken sleep. Gin was a just-screwed-in metal plate across his forehead, and he could taste everyone from Winnie's Grill's cigarettes way up in his nose.

"This ain't cute," he muttered to the empty room.

Little things, like the thrill on the rare occasion that he saw a new part of Richmond, made him think that the world was bigger than just apartment, museum security five days a week, and Winnie's Grill on weekends, plus the occasional Karaoke Wednesday. Knowing that something else was out there kept him up at night sometimes. If he could find that place, do that thing, then he could figure everything out. He kicked the covers off his legs, powerful from climbing museum stairs, then swiveled his butt on the mattress and clomped across the bare floor, excited to see his family. At least he had them.

Paul had the type of hangover that craved food more wholesome than he would ever make at home. In the bathroom, splashing cold water on his face and massaging his temples with his fingertips, he listened to an engine turning over on the block and took mental stock of what he had in the refrigerator. The thought of leftover Chinese chicken and broccoli clenched his gut, but he walked into the kitchenette, trailing his right hand along the counter that separated it from the living room.

Paul's apartment is tidy because he doesn't have

a lot of stuff to make a mess with. The living room wall has a 1970s-style, triangle mirror with three small shelves. The top one is dusty, with an old incense holder and a framed photo of Paul sitting at a picnic table between grade school-age Kevin and Laura. The longest shelf is in the middle and has a row of VHS tapes anchored by two high school track trophies. On the bottom, a purple-streaked rock from the Maryland shore, a miniature green Buddha, two books by James Baldwin, and a ticket stub from a Mariah Carey concert.

In the morning, the front of the apartment gets enough sun that the lights can stay off. The natural glow masks the butter-thick layer of dust on the windowsill above the kitchen sink. The window had been open all night, and cool air mixed with the chemical chill of the open fridge. And there it was, on a Styrofoam plate next to a bag of red grapes, a full quarter of Winnie's red velvet cake, with a fingertip-wide ditch slashed across the frosting on top like an arrow pointing out at Paul.

At the sight of the cake, Paul filled with that same warm, hopeful feeling that he'd had in the car. He set it on the counter. The silverware drawer jingled open like a cash register, and Paul held a fork in the air. After taking a deep breath, relishing his view of the beet-red cake, Paul plunged the fork in and lowered his eyelids as he brought that first bite to his mouth.

He waited to be transported to a time of lemonade, not gin. Of the airy rowhouse on Marshall St., not this apartment. Of his first job doing deliveries for the pharmacy on 2nd St., not the museum where the polished linoleum floors hurt his lower back.

Paul inhaled and squished the cake against the roof of his mouth. It was lousy. Stale, with crumbs that sucked away his saliva. The frosting was pasty, sticking to his gums, and the cake tasted like sugar and sour cigarettes, spoiled by the air in Winnie's.

Paul's eyes popped open, and his whole body stiffened before pivoting to the sink and spitting out the bite with a *Ptuuwuh!*

"Ah, hell. Let's go to Sheila's," he told the faucet, slurping water before dressing in less than five minutes.

As he pulled the maroon LeBaron off his block, sending a breeze up the back of a slow-walking church woman in a lime green hat, he smelled fruity liquor mingling with the sandalwood and hide of his leather jacket and remembered Xavier's Alize. Paul smiled and felt the transmission's pleasant thump as it switched into third gear.

You ever see one of those movies where teenagers sleep until noon on the weekend? Well, I wish I lived in one of those movies because Mama always comes knocking around 9:30 saying, "Let's make this day happen."

This Sunday, though, the smell of bacon beat Mama to the punch. She just about only cooks bacon when Grandpa comes by, so I lay in bed for a minute, wondering what was up. I heard a spatula ding the side of the skillet that Mama saves for what she calls, "Country Cookin'." It's wack as hell when she says that, because we live in Richmond, and the most country thing around is the "Are-you-ready-for-some-football" redneck BS that my PE teacher Mr. B blasts in his pick-up truck when he drives by the buses after school. Mama's wack, but she ain't that wack. She's just not country.

Quiet voices drifted upstairs. Mama and a man. Mama was talking fast and light, pausing every now and then to let the man laugh. I recognized that laugh. It was Uncle Paul. He's got a chuckle that sounds like water bubbling down the drain. He's the man.

Uncle Paul has an earring. I used to think earrings were gay, but then a bunch of rappers got their ears pierced. Not long after, Uncle Paul got an earring and that sealed the deal—I wanted one too, but Mama said I had to wait until I was eighteen. Forever.

Uncle Paul wears a small gold hoop in his left ear that matches his gold glasses, which look cool. Paul can even make glasses look cool. That never happens.

The stuff he wears always matches. The earring and the glasses. The leather hat to go with the smooth, zip-up leather coat.

Sometimes Mama jokes that Paul's another son of hers since he doesn't have a wife or kids, and he always raids the fridge when he comes by. That'd be fine by me. I wish he lived here.

I sat up in bed and ran my hand up the back of my head. My haircut was still jacked up, and I knew Uncle Paul would clown me. I didn't want to get clowned, even though when Paul did it, it felt like he was joking instead of cracking, you know? I put on a hoodie and left the hood dangling off the back of my head, then went downstairs before the bacon disappeared.

Uncle Paul was sitting sideways at the kitchen table, leaned against the wall, sipping coffee and nodding at Mama at the stove. I walked careful to keep my hood on, and when he spotted me, he broke into his gap-toothed, Cheshire grin.

"Big K!"

He was wearing his leather coat that smelled like sweet wood. The zipper dug into my wrist when he stood to clasp hands, clap me on the back, and give me a quick hug. Of course, he didn't waste any time flicking off my hood and saying, "Let's see this 'haircut' of yours."

He leaned in frowning, fake-serious, picked at a bit of hair on my neckline and said, "Hooo goodness. This lint gonna come off?"

Usually, I wouldn't take that kind of mess, but Uncle Paul was different, and I wanted some bacon. I said good morning to him and Mama, even though I wasn't too hyped on seeing her.

Another cool thing about Paul is that he puts Mama in a good mood, and she starts acting fun and younger. Mama doesn't stay mad much anyway, she just lets it all out when it needs to happen.

Mama said, "Hey Kevin. You're up just on time. I was gonna come knock and wake you up."

"I smelled bacon," I said.

Uncle Paul laughed and sat back down. "I did too. I was driving by, and had to hit the brake when I smelled your mama's cooking."

Mama said, "Shut up, boy," and flicked the spatula at Paul. A booger of egg catapulted off the spatula and landed on my sleeve. Before I could think, I swiped it off with my middle finger and went, "The hell is wrong with you, Mama?"

Then, I realized what I'd said and stuck the eggy finger in my mouth, waiting to get grounded all over again. But Mama rolled her eyes at Uncle Paul and said, "You see what I mean?" and I noticed that they both had their lips screwed up, trying not to laugh. I started to get my back up at them laughing at me, but if they thought it was funny, I knew I'd still get some bacon, so I looked into the skillet to calm myself down. The bacon looked like super-long Band-Aids.

Mama reached over to the sink and flipped me the sponge, which left a wet rectangle on the front of my hoodie when I caught it. She said, "There you go, Kevin. 'My bad,'" then raised an eyebrow at Uncle Paul, thinking she's so clever for using one of me and Laura's expressions. "Kevin, part of your punishment is that…"

I opened my mouth to say something because I was sick of them laughing at me, and now she was trying to change my punishment.

She stuck a finger in the air, like "One minute," then started again, slower. Out the corner of my eye, I saw Uncle Paul settle back into his chair to watch.

"…part of your punishment is that you've gotta go out with Uncle Paul for a while today."

Right away, my hand flew up to my raggedy head. What if some girls saw me?

"He's taking you to the barber, Kevin."

I went to town on four pieces of bacon, three scrambled eggs with cheese, a glass of OJ, and two slices of toasted Wonder Bread that got chewy from all the butter and grape jelly, then I ran upstairs to get cleaned up. The barber. All this time I'd been asking to go to the barber. To get a fade. To get a Gumbi. And here I was about to go, and the way it happened was I got grounded? That didn't make any sense, but I wasn't about to fuss.

I was in a real rush and busted into the bathroom with my hoodie half off. Laura was in there in a baby blue bra, looking in the mirror with her butt poking out over half a circle of makeup bottles and hair products on the toilet seat.

She screamed like she'd just seen Dracula. I went, "Oh dang!" and tried to grab the doorknob, but my arm was stuck in my hoodie so I lost my balance and fell to my knees. Laura marched across the bathroom floor with her left arm over her breasts, yelling, "Get out of here. You nasty. Get out!"

She kicked her toes right into my buttcrack, and I rolled out the bathroom. The door slammed behind me, and I made a beeline into my room and fell face-first across my bed. I'm always thinking about what I'd do to see a girl with no shirt on, but the closest I've come so far is my sister in a bra. Nasty.

Uncle Paul drove with the windows up. It was like cruising in a warm, leather jacket bubble with coconut-shaped air fresheners jiggling off the rearview mirror when he took a turn. Paul's seats were soft corduroy, and I slouched down and watched Richmond roll by from under the brim of my Braves hat, nodding a bit to the drum hits just coming through on the radio.

Mama would have been going on about work or grades or something, but me and Paul didn't even have to talk. We just vibed to the music, Paul tapping out the beat on the steering wheel and glancing into the rearview. I've got some rotten luck being stuck with Mama and Laura, and wish I could live with Paul. He's got a decent-sized apartment. I could sleep on the couch, and it wouldn't be weird to bring a girl over. If I ever brought a girl home now, I know Mama would break out the drawing I got in trouble for in third grade, when I tried to draw muscles on an Indian's chest, but they wound up looking like breasts.

We went to a barber near downtown, where the houses are closer together. The shop was the last on a small, low strip of businesses by a stoplight. Singing and jingling tambourines came from the church next door. Across the alley on the other side was a square, cinderblock building, covered in thick, turquoise paint, with posters for different albums in the window, plus a faded Malcolm X t-shirt on a hanger.

We sat on some folding chairs by the barbershop's glass door, next to half a dozen guys who were waiting for haircuts, too. The shop was long and narrow, with mirrors and barber chairs along the left wall. The air was full of the hum of clippers, the smell of baby powder, and the deep, grumbling voices that men use on each other. The only woman had two little boys who kept fidgeting around. The younger one kept crying, and the mother, who didn't look much older than Laura, smacked him on the hand and yelled, "You ain't gonna get no candy if you keep on like that, Ervin."

As soon as her slap landed on him, it was like she'd twisted the volume knob up, and he roared for a second until he realized he wasn't getting more attention. I was kinda staring and imagining the mother having sex to make those babies when she looked up, lips flattened, and I looked away. An old school show was playing on the boombox on the table in the corner. I recognized the song that Biggie used for "Big Poppa" and started nodding my head like I'd been grooving to the music all along.

"You like the Isleys, Kevin?" Uncle Paul asked, looking surprised.

At first, I thought the family with the trashy mama slapping her boy were named the Isleys, but that didn't seem right. Then Paul sang along with the radio in a high voice, "Between the sheets."

"Oh, yeah, yeah," I said.

"I know your mama plays this at home some-times, right?"

"Ha. Yeah."

She actually didn't play that one. It would suck to be stuck at home with Mama listening to a song called "Between the Sheets." I wondered if Paul had a girlfriend to get between the sheets with.

There were only two barbers. At the chair by the door was a middle-aged guy with a clean, bald head and a just-clipped, triangle mustache who took steady steps on his feet, moving the razor around customers' heads, then chasing it with the scissors before buffing their cuts with a big, powdery brush.

The other barber was a lot younger. He was light-skinned and chubby with an earring in each ear. His cheeks were so big that his features were all scrunched into the middle of his face. Under his apron, he wore a half-unbuttoned, shiny, red shirt. He had the sides of his hair faded down with a little curly line shaved up off of his neckline. The top of his hair had a greasy curl, and bits of it were bleached orange. He held the clippers with a bent wrist and led with his neck as he moved them over his customer. He might have been gay.

The little boy who'd just got slapped was still making shuddering, snuffling sounds with his nose.

The younger barber looked at him and said, "We'll get you calm as a lil' cat once you're in this chair."

"Boy, what *you* know about *cat*?" asked the older barber, who barked a laugh and went back to snipping the scissors.

The young mother threw her neck out and said, "'scuse me?"

A fat guy in a purple sweatsuit that made him look like Grimace from McDonald's piped in and said, "Settle down, now. What Saul meant was that Xavier…prefers dogs."

Xavier went, "Mmm-hmm."

Grimace stood up to slap a friend five, and I kept watching because I felt like I'd missed something, but wished I had friends like that to joke with. You watch TV and it's always a crew of four or five people who hang out all the time and have a bunch of jokes and stories, but real life is never like that.

"I'm sorry, ma'am. Why don't you and your boys take next on my chair?" asked the older barber. When the mother led her sons to his chair, the younger barber smiled and nodded at us, extending a hand to his empty chair. Paul clapped me on the back and said, "Take a seat."

I didn't know about sitting in this guy's chair. What if someone from school passed by and saw him touching my head and thought we were gay together? Then again, this barber looked like he knew more about the types of haircuts young people got. Who knows what you'd get from an old, bald barber.

I got in the chair. The barber draped the cloth around my neck, whipped off my hat and said, "What do we have here?"

With a mirror right in front of me, I got a good look at just how messed up my cut was. There were patches coming off the top of my head, and the right side was longer, like someone had knocked me in the left ear and pushed more hair out the other side. Along with that, my forehead had a line from my hat, and there was a new zit between my eyes. In the mirror, I saw the barber handing my hat to Uncle Paul, who'd gotten all smiley. He looked proud. Maybe I should mess up my hair more often.

"We need to get this cleaned up, Xavier," said Paul. "But we don't have much left to work with. What kind of cut do you want, Kevin?"

He looked at me in the mirror. I looked up at the barber, who was wiping off his clippers. How did Paul know this guy's name?

I said, "A fade," in a tough voice to prove I wasn't gay and that I came to the barber all the time.

"Alright now, we can do that," said Xavier, squinting in and running three fingers above my left ear. Up close, he had a deep, oily smell, topped off with cinnamon gum and fruity shampoo or something. I got mad that the barber was touching me all close, but it also tickled, and I had to make myself not scrunch in my shoulders, and that made me have to piss a little.

The cut took no time. First, Xavier moved around me, taking it all down to one length, checking the cut, then the reflection in the mirror, making shorter layers of hair until he reached skin an inch above my ears.

Uncle Paul chimed in, "Did you know that his mama usually cuts his hair?"

Xavier opened his mouth to say something wise, but I mean-mugged him, and all he said was, "Oh. Is that so?"

"Uh-huh," Paul continued, "But yesterday, my man Kevin decided to take matters into his own hands."

Paul's voice rose into a high chuckle, and he slapped his magazine on his knee. At the next chair, the older boy's eyes were glazed over, and he was working a sucker like a baby bottle while getting his cut. It reminded me of the hair on my bed, and I wondered how many curls would stick to the kid's candy.

Xavier did a little humming laugh and shook his head while snapping a different guard on the clippers.

"We all gotta take matters into our own hands sometimes. So, how you know his mama, Paul?"

Paul jumped right back and said, "'cause she my

sister, Xavier. What you thought?"

They laughed. I closed my eyes and thought about how I needed to get around men more often so I could have these conversations. Xavier nudged the clippers across my front hairline. After he brushed my forehead, I opened my eyes and looked in the mirror. The fade was perfect, spraying down the sides of my head like graffiti. Xavier used the side of the razor to cut a half-moon on the right side of the top, and I started cheesing in the mirror.

Beyond Xavier, Uncle Paul was nodding his head with the magazine in his lap. Xavier unclasped the cloth and motioned to Paul to take the chair.

"Naw, I'm good for now," Paul said.

"You sure you're good? I'm surprised to see you up and about this early, Paul," Xavier raised his eyebrows in the mirror. Paul inhaled and shook his head.

"Hey, it's never too early for some QT with my nephew."

I smiled, then Xavier looked at me in the mirror and went, "QT?" Then faster, "QT... *Cutie* is right."

Uncle Paul started to laugh into his leather wallet, and it took me a minute to get the joke. At first, I wanted to join in laughing, then my ears got hot, and I glared at their reflections. How was Paul gonna let him talk about me like that?

Me, Uncle Paul, and my new haircut hit a McDonald's drive-thru, and I knew it was a good day because they gave me both sauces I ordered, barbecue and honey mustard. I looked out the car window at people on the street and tried to guess how fresh their cuts were. None of them had just been to the barber. It made me want to dangle out the window, hollering. I'd never been fresher than everyone else.

The warm, greasy fries smell filled the car. Paul flicked a switch to roll down the windows, then pumped the radio, so the singer mixed with the wind. It had turned into a really nice day, clear and sunny. The right day to be out, cheating at being grounded.

We took Broad St. through downtown, past the tall hospital buildings, then up to the cool, old houses in Church Hill. At the top of the hill, Uncle Paul revved the engine, the car jumped forward, and my straw scraped the roof of my mouth. I tapped it with my tongue, tasted blood, blinked, and turned to say something. Paul cackled and went, "We gotta hurry. Can't let that McDonald's get cold."

He cut a right into Chimborazo Park and muttered, "Nothing worse than cold McDonald's."

Chimborazo is a site from the Civil War, and the city made it a park. It's to the side of the road, and after a block it stops at a cliff that looks back over downtown and the chocolate milk-colored river. Paul pointed the car out over the train tracks and woods under the cliff. Everything got quiet when he cut the engine, so I rustled the McDonald's bag as I passed it to him. He looked into the bag, smiling and pushing his hat back on his head. I decided that when I'm grown, I'm not going to dress all boring either. I'll dress like Paul, with a leather coat and maybe some turtlenecks. Not church clothes. Clothes that make you look smart, but like you can still get down.

While he was unwrapping his sandwich, Paul asked, "How's your sister doing? Still hung up on that Corey?"

Over Thanksgiving, Laura caught her boyfriend Corey getting with her best friend Sharese at a party. That was when Saturday Night Laura started making appearances at home, with bright, new shades of nail polish and attitude to match.

"Laura's alright. I dunno about Corey. She doesn't have a new boyfriend or nothin', but I haven't heard her playing that Jodeci tape much either."

Paul threw back his head and laughed, then brought his face back down, still showing some teeth.

"Jodeci," he said, then chuckled and shook his head. What was up with that? Ain't nothing funny about Jodeci. Just some guys whining songs about girls. I looked at the river and threw two chicken nuggets in my mouth.

"Food alright?" Paul asked. He had a fish sandwich and some nuggets open in his lap like they were telling him what they wanted for Christmas.

I was still chewing when I said, "McDonald's is McDonald's. An' I like it."

Paul nodded and said, "Me too," then did a quick switch, looking out over the river. "You been getting along with your mama?"

I knew she'd told Paul about yesterday even though it wasn't really his business. But maybe Paul had some ideas.

"Usually. Except every now and then when she gets all…you know." I dipped a fry into the whirlpool of sauces in the top of the nuggets' box. I couldn't tell Uncle Paul that Mama acted "bitchy," because Mama's his sister, and, well, she's my mama.

"I know it's not easy where you're at. When I was in seventh grade, your grandma was on my back all the time. If I got a B, it was 'Why's it not a A?' If I went out, she didn't like who I was hanging out with." He picked up his drink. "But if I stayed home, she wondered why I ain't had any friends. Man." He snorted into his soda.

This all sounded familiar. But just because Paul had to deal with it didn't mean it was alright. I looked at the river water making white foam around a big rock.

"Why she gotta be like that, Uncle Paul?"

Paul wiped the sides of his cup with a yellow napkin, put it back in the drink holder in front of the stereo, and tilted his head back, squinting out at Southside.

"You're gonna think I'm trippin', but it's because she's your mama, and she loves you. And her way of loving you is to worry about you." He turned to me. "Which just might drive you crazy."

"Phew."

"I know, man. I know," Paul rapped the top of the steering wheel with his open hand. "But look, you gotta be careful around your mama. She's at that age." Paul waved his head back and forth, trying to shake the right words loose. "That age where her body starts changing." He raised his eyebrows and gave me a know-what-I'm-sayin' look, then went on, slowly. "And she might feel different, you know? It might make her more *sensitive* to things."

What was he talking about?

"Something you should know, Kevin, if you're starting to," Paul took his hand off the wheel and pointed a thumb out the window behind him, "get out there, is that, you can't say nothing bad about a lady's appearance."

I definitely wanted to "get out there," but when he looked me in the eye, there was a terrible second where I thought about Mama's appearance, at home in sweatpants and that yellow t-shirt from the church cookout, and how she must have looked good to someone sometime because that's how me and Laura got here. Nasty. I squeezed my soda cup to keep it from slipping down my fingers and stayed quiet. This type of stuff is never easy to talk about, but I was hoping it'd be easier with Paul.

"Think what you like, and talk about it with your boys. Just, if you want an easier time, keep it to yourself around the ladies," he said.

Paul knew a lot about women, and this was making sense. Still, I didn't like that Mama could say what she wanted, but I couldn't say nothing to her. But she wasn't there, and I was out with Uncle Paul, some good lunch, and a fresh haircut. Which reminded me to ask, "Hey, Uncle Paul?"

He stopping balling up the blue and yellow sandwich wrapper in his hand and looked over at me. I suddenly got embarrassed and checked my haircut in the rearview.

"What's wrong, Kevin?"

"Do my haircut make me look gay?"

Paul's face froze with his mouth a quarter open, then he looked back out the windshield and sighed through his nose. My heart filled my throat. What if Paul thought the haircut was gay, but was about to lie and say no?

A car drove by playing Craig Mack, but I didn't nod

my head. Finally, still watching the river, Paul asked, "Why would a haircut make you look gay?"

"Well, I know it's not, like, a gay haircut, but… that barber. He was gay, right?"

It felt weird to say "gay" out loud in this way, not making fun of people. Just talking. I remembered the girly, curly-fingered way that the barber had held the clippers. I wasn't sure I'd been around gay dudes before, and this guy had given me an ill fade. What if I just thought the fade was ill because I was gay too? I couldn't be! I'd get jumped all the time and never get any girls.

Paul shrugged and said, "It's a nice haircut. Real clean."

It was. Paul said, "It looks like the same haircut I've seen on a lot of guys. That shop wasn't that busy, so they didn't all get their cuts there. And I doubt all the barbers in Richmond are gay…"

"Wait, so he was gay?"

I held my soda six inches from my face. What if someone from school saw this fade and knew it was gay? Did I just do something gay by accident? I sunk down in my seat.

Paul shook his head and drummed on the steering wheel, one-two-three, then said, "That's not the point, Kevin. You got a good haircut."

Neither of us spoke. I usually like how Uncle Paul's got it all figured out, but this time, it was starting to tick me off. The treetops below waved as a breeze passed through them. Paul pointed out the driver's side window to a little road that snaked under the park's cliff and said, "You know what that area used to be called?"

I spread a hand over the top of my head, sat up and looked out. "No."

Paul lifted his head and said, "Sugar Bottom," shaking his chin like he was talking about a legendary thing.

"Sugar Bottom?" So?

"Yeah," Paul said, nodding kinda fast.

"Why?" I slurped my soda down to ice.

"Because, back in the day, that area used to be full of hookers, and jazz cats would go there," Paul flicked his eyebrows up and down and his hat wiggled too, "to get some sugar."

"Ohh." I looked again, imagining naked, old-timey, jazz ladies falling out of the trees.

"Ain't no one down there now. Any of those hookers still alive, they probably older than my grandmama," he said.

We both pulled sour faces at the idea of an old lady hooker. I kept looking at Sugar Bottom as Paul cut the car on and reversed out the inlet. Mama never would have told me about that. Or she might have, and it would have been nasty.

After *The Simpsons*, I went in the bathroom to check out my fade, then flipped over Mama's hand mirror and held it like a mic, pretending to do comedy on TV. The camera was catching my cut from each side while the crowd of dressed-up people rolled in their seats, laughing at me tiptoeing across the stage, telling a joke about a gay barber.

I caught my own eye in the mirror and tried to give a cool smile like Larenz Tate. He could show teeth and not look goofy. Girls like that.

Would Aisha like my cut? The only reason I like Science Lab is because Aisha sits by me. She's mixed or something, with orangey hair and a mouth that's was always puckered, whistling easy air. Sometimes, I see her tan hand with sparkling, purple nail polish running over my back, but it's a version of my back with so many muscles that I look like a goddamn armadillo, and there's twinkly keyboards playing because we're in some R&B video that Laura would watch.

Aisha looks like she's sitting in a hot tub when she's riding my bus because her Adidases are on the seat and her back is wedged into the corner by the window. She's telling Janelle with the Toni Braxton pixie cut, "I'm going to Kevin's," and that eye-rolling gossip don't dare laugh.

Those things are always just right because they're in my head. In real life, she's so perfect that I don't even know where to start with the talking. Once or twice, I got on a roll making jokes and saying words that came from I don't know where, but most days, I look at her until she says, "Hi." Then, I nod and say "Hi" back and feel myself growing tall out my British Knights.

In real life, Aisha touches my arm when she laughs at a *Simpsons* joke, and I kiss that part of my arm during the slice of time after school when I'm glad to be alone, before I'm sick of being alone.

I wish we could stand under a tree while I touched her all four times that she's touched me. Maybe she'd look me in the eye, and I'd kiss her, and the tree would turn into a bedroom, and we'd get it on with condoms that magically appeared so we wouldn't get AIDS or nothing. This could happen sometime when Demetric wasn't there to point and hoot if she pushed my hand away. Maybe this ill fade would change that. Just don't let her find out where I got the cut.

CHAPTER 3: MONDAY

1

Kevin

Me and David have been tight since the first week of first grade. He was the new kid at school and people from around Battery Park were walking home and asking him questions.

"Where you from?"

"Southside," David answered.

"Why you moved?"

"Mama found a place with a bedroom for me."

Even then, he talked fast, like he was mad people didn't already know.

Tyrell, who was only eight feet tall back then, snuck up and unzipped David's backpack a couple inches each time he took a step. We all snuck looks while David walked ahead, sure of himself. When we got to the top of the hill by Battery Park, Tyrell asked David, "Can they run on Southside?"

"Yeah."

"Then let's race down the hill. Finish line at the tree on the corner."

David yelled, "Go!" and took off running, legs kicking in the air, face leaned out to the finish line, tongue of his backpack flapping. A neon palm tree Trapper Keeper slapped to the sidewalk, and David shot away with his elbows pumping faster than his legs. Next came a metal, Muppets lunchbox that busted open, so Tyrell had to hop over the Thermos rolling on the sidewalk.

David won by three steps because Tyrell kept turning to the rest of us and pointing when something fell out of David's bag. We all smiled but didn't laugh too loud. If we did, David would notice. If we did, it would get Tyrell's attention, and we'd be next.

David hopped off the curb, turned and stood in the middle of the street, smiling back up the hill until Tyrell zipped past yelling, "You dropped something," as he disappeared into the park, hooting.

A car at the stop sign honked at David. His face fell when he saw the trail of stuff up the sidewalk. The other kids pointed and laughed, but I hung back, stopping every couple steps to pick up David's things. At the bottom of the hill, I had a pile of school supplies and a new friend. Yeah, I'd laughed with everyone else, but it was because I was glad Tyrell was pulling that trick on someone besides me.

Tyrell was in the second grade then, but he should have been in third. By the time we got to third grade, Tyrell was there for the second time, but he stopped bothering us after Laura slapped him on the ear twice with her hairbrush after he tried to pants me in the handball line at recess. Laura's good like that.

Things are different now, since me, David, and Tyrell are in seventh grade, and Laura's in high school. Going to school sucks enough. Imagine having to go to school for longer by being in the same grade twice. What about the first day when you have to be the new kid in class because everyone else is a year younger than you? Like, "'sup little babies. I was born in the '70s. Disco inferno!"

What about when you ran into people from your grade the year before, and they treated you like a scrub because you got held back? Like, "'sup, re-re. You gonna learn to r-e-a-d this time around?"

Maybe that's why Tyrell's so mean, but then again, he was like that before he ever got held back, so I don't know.

Man, I bet his teachers were mad to see him again.

Now, Tyrell is friends with these other big dudes named Leo and Spayne. I think they met at a special summer camp for thugs who got held back. Instead of kickball or swimming, they practiced breaking into lockers and cornering people for money. I know it's messed up, but that sounds fun, and I wish I could have learned it with them so I'd be on their side, instead of being stuck with geeky David. I mean, David will always be there on the block, but we're at a new school, and I wish my locker was next to someone besides him, maybe a cooler guy who knows some girls and doesn't have an ashy chalkboard neck.

Our school's old. When you first walk in, there are class photos from the '50s to now. The school was segregated before Martin Luther King, so the pictures from the '50s and '60s are all white people wearing funny-shaped glasses and sitting on corncobs. By the '70s, there are a few black people in the pictures with big 'fros and beaded necklaces like pictures of Mama in high school. They're bits of pepper in a salt spill. But it's reversed by 1980, and the pictures look like Oreo cookies—mainly black, with a little white in the middle.

The stairs to the second floor have grooves worn into them from being walked on for fifty years. That's where me and David were on Monday morning when we saw Tyrell and his crew half a flight up, milling around in a ball of noise and bookbags. We ducked in behind this big girl Denise who was puffing out breaths as she went up one step at a time. I'd have to pay for pouring water on Tyrell, but why hurry?

Tyrell yelled, "You gets one, man!" at Leo and shoved him against the railing. The whole school shook as Leo crumpled against the wall, laughing. Frizzy-braids Spayne stopped on the step above them and pointed, shouting, "Aww!"

People tiptoed past on the left side of the stairs.

Leo pushed himself off the wall and slapped off Tyrell's red and blue Braves hat. It spun through the air like a UFO and landed against the other railing. A folded-up bill fell out and dropped three stairs. This kid Chauncey, who wears Coke bottle glasses and smells like tartar sauce, hopped so he wouldn't step on Tyrell's hat. The stairs got quiet. If the hat was messed up, someone was gonna get messed up to go along with it.

Tyrell stuck an arm out to block traffic, and if it was a movie, there would have been a quiet drumroll as he bent to pick up the hat and brush it off. The cymbal crashed, and everyone let out a breath as he put the hat on his head and turned upstairs. I smiled because he hadn't noticed the dropped money, a five, in front of my right foot. Everyone melted away in a rush as I bent my knee and scooped the bill into my hoodie pocket. I was proud because I expect myself to be that smooth, but I usually don't get the chance to act like it.

The bill felt rough in my hand. I looked at David trailing his hand along the railing with his eyebrows knitted up, scared for my health. Tyrell's crew disappeared into the second floor, and the noise from their carrying on got cut off as the doors swung shut behind them. David kept quiet until we got to our lockers on the next floor up.

"You shouldn't have taken that money, Kevin."

He was leaning around my open locker door, speaking low, fast and serious.

"Why?"

"What if he finds out?"

He wouldn't even say Tyrell's name.

"How's he gonna find out? No one saw, right?"

The five grew hot in my kangaroo pocket, magic money that could grow huge and pop out in front of Tyrell. I palmed the bill and dropped it in my jeans pocket.

David said, "I don't know. Someone might have. Or he might catch on if you go around school spending money or something." David shook his left hand, holding an imaginary five-dollar bill.

"It's five dollars. It's not like I'll be high rolling! Besides, what was I supposed to do? Leave it for someone else?"

I could just see some scrub like Tameka finding it and saying, "What kind of fool gonna step over some money?"

I'm no fool.

"You coulda given it back to him."

"Yeah, I could just see that." I checked behind me real quick to make sure Tyrell wasn't there, then put on a goodie-two-shoes voice and said, "Here ya go, Mr. Tyrell sir. You dropped this money, and I just had to return it to its rightful owner."

David said, "It's not too late." He reminded me of those Save the Children ads on TV.

I slammed his locker door, which sent him stumbling, and said, "Let's just get us some extra lunch at the cafeteria today."

David perked up and said, "Lunch, huh?"

David's a little guy, but he eats enough for three big guys. His mama wasn't working last summer, and she'd always send him to our place around lunchtime. After two days and half a pack of cheese slices, Laura told Mama, who told me not to say nothing because she didn't want to embarrass Ms. Gunderson, even though she called her "tacky." Instead, Mama told Laura to put less baloney on the sandwiches and cover it up with extra mustard when David came over. The idea of someone messing with my baloney ticked me off, so I stopped letting David come by for lunch, but I never told him why.

"Yeah, I'll get at you in the cafeteria."

David whispered, "But Tyrell's in our lunch."

"What's he gonna do? Recognize Lincoln's face?"

All morning, I felt the corner of the five poking my thigh through my pocket. It felt like a hundred. I dipped my leg because it had turned into a heavy roll, to be peeled off as needed to give to fine girls.

It felt good to have that money, and I got so deep into my strut that I walked past Aisha's locker, number 216, with half a mind to draw a heart on the five and slip it through the vents on the door. It'd glow red like a Coke machine and a firehose of hearts would burst out when she went to get her science book after lunch.

Being grounded during the week ain't all that bad because I only miss a couple hours of fun after school. But, knowing my luck, the five would make Aisha stick her hand on the wall by my locker and go, "Hey Kevin, wanna roll by after school today? They got a rerun of *Sister, Sister* on."

Then, I'd have to make up some excuse about going to the doctor to get my muscles checked out because they won't stop being swole. But I'm not that slick. I'd probably slam my locker door and go, "Dammit, I'm grounded! I'm never gonna get any action."

Then she'd step back and say, "A'ight, loser. Peace."

The heels of her Adidases would disappear as I stared at the floor tiles, fuming through my nose.

By the time I got my bookbag on my shoulder, Aisha would be walking by with caterpillar-eyebrows Demetric, and it'd be one of the days when he wore his big brother's football jersey. Wish I had a big brother. Wish I was in high school.

I'd ask, "Maybe next week?"

"Yeah right. If your mama say it's cool."

Then she'd turn to Demetric and ask him, "Anyone ever say you look like that fine Larenz Tate?"

"Yeah."

For real, though. If Aisha asked me to kick it, I'd go. What would Mama do, ground me all over again? No TV for a week would be A-OK if I could sit on the couch and think, *Tongues are strawberry-ish because they're slippery and gritty. Makeup feels powdery? Oily? under your finger. Her stomach is smooth as the back of a spoon across ice cream. You unhook a bra by rubbing your fingertips like the world's tiniest violin. A titty feels like a Nerf ball a titty feels like a water balloon a titty feels like a beanbag chair.*

3
Paul

For fifteen seconds of seventh grade, Paul was alone with Ronald's ass. Paul had never paid attention to Ronald until the day the short boy had to write on the board in math. To reach the numerator with the chalk, he stood on his tiptoes and pointed his butt out for balance. Paul had only been watching because he was bored and glad he hadn't been called up, but then the butt caught his attention. Two red grapes under Ronald's chinos, bobbing a bit as he wrote on the board.

That year, guys had been talking about girls. Paul talked about girls, too. He always felt like he was saying what needed to be said to be part of the conversation and hoping that if he kept saying it, he'd mean it. Once, he'd even tried to start the talk on his own, walking back from school and telling one of the boys, "I wanna bite Pan Logan's titties."

The boy had just looked at Paul, who felt his face growing hot as he imagined the taste of breasts in his mouth, the blood that might seep out if he bit them, full of seeds and pulp like a ripe tomato.

That day in math, Paul imagined himself sitting at a small, round table at a jazzy lounge that his grandfather might have gone to back when. A red curtain whisked aside to reveal Ronald, stretching as far as he could to write at the top of a blackboard while raunchy, brass blues played from the wings.

Paul wanted to slap Ronald's ass. He wanted to press his hand into it. He wanted to kneel in front of Ronald, hook his hand between the young man's legs and give his ass a firm hug. After that, Paul snuck looks at other boys' butts as they ran in PE class or bent to reach into their lockers.

One evening, he looked at his Pop's butt as he stood at the phone in the kitchen, growling, "Shoot, Henry. Car ain't fixed, ain't gonna drive," and laughing as the last bit of sun glinted off his beer can. Even the beer looked cold and sharp, dangerous in his father's hand. Paul looked away.

He wished he had sunglasses that he could wear indoors like Rick James might do. Deep, black pools to cover his eyes so they could roam, noting the sizes and shapes of butts that wiggled into his field of vision, guessing their softness. He wanted to get a pair of shades and switch schools, showing up wearing them on the first day so everyone would think he was a blind kid. So he could look without worrying about being caught and getting called "Sissy." So he wouldn't have to take notes in class.

He tried looking at girls. Tried to break the hold that men had on him. But it didn't work. Girls were too soft. Lacking power and subtlety. It was then that Paul knew he was different, but it was a while before he could admit just how different he was.

It's strange. Years later, once he knew that he liked men—Yeah, liked men. Not gay. Not a sissy. Not a faggot. Maybe a homosexual, if you want to sound like a doctor—Paul realized one of the things that had been holding him back. Aside from the fear of beatings, or the fear of losing friends and family, he was worried that if he admitted to himself that he was gay, he would turn super feminine. His wrists would go limp, and he'd start sashaying and bugging his eyes like Little Richard. But that never happened, and Paul always wanted to tell people, *Just because I like men doesn't make me any different than I was before you knew.*

And that's when he became Steady Paul.

Steady Paul is not a limp-wristed scream queen. Steady Paul does not throw confetti everywhere and roll his neck. Steady Paul does not care what color the drapes are or do two snaps up in a z-formation. Steady Paul is a man like any other, maybe even manlier than others. He is the broad-shouldered museum security guard who helps lost kids find their parents and keeps teenagers on school trips from touching the displays and each other. Steady Paul is who Uncle Paul becomes when he doesn't want anyone asking any of the wrong questions.

Steady Paul was good but had secrets that he couldn't share for fear of Steady Paul crumpling to the floor like a popped balloon. That kept him from getting close to most people. And that was getting to be a problem as the people he was close to who only knew him as Steady Paul were getting old enough to ask questions. What would Kevin do if he found out? It wasn't violence that Paul feared. It was losing this relationship that he'd been cultivating since he was a teenager and Kevin was a baby. It would all mean nothing if he couldn't be honest with his own family, with this kid that he thought the world of.

Paul flexed his shoulders down and took on a blank expression, turning himself into Steady Paul as he hustled down the block to old Mrs. Williams' house. This time, her call had been mysterious: "Paul? I need you here."

He buttoned his shirt as he crossed the street, picturing the old lady who had given him one of her dead husband's suits (too old-timey and Cab Calloway-looking), whose oven pilot he lit, lying on the floor like those "I've fallen and I can't get up" commercials.

He tried the door handle, then knocked. She answered in lime green slacks and a blouse that had turned yellow since it had been in fashion. Paul realized that if she had been hurt on her kitchen floor, she couldn't have reached her phone, or answered the door.

"Come in, Paul," Mrs. Williams said, shuffling back and pulling the door open.

By now, Mrs. Williams would have said what needed doing. She was a retired schoolteacher who always got right down to business. He stepped inside, breathed in mothballs and yesterday's baked chicken, then asked, "What's going on?"

A wicked smile split her face as she pushed the door shut and pointed into the living room. He turned, expecting to see the TV askew on its stand, and she said, "I want you to meet my grand-niece, Izola. She's down visiting from Howard."

Izola was like a sunspot in the middle of a photo. She sat on the dusty couch in a flowered, blue dress, the steam from a cup of tea rippling the air in front of her. Longish legs, which Paul liked. Hair in a ponytail. Kinda big teeth that she covered with the teacup half a second after she smiled. Nice looking woman with a girl next door vibe. Paul felt drawn to her like they already shared a joke.

Mrs. Williams shut the door, placed a hand on the small of his back, and aimed him at the couch. He stumbled forward, nodding at Izola and redirecting himself toward the deceased Mr. Williams' armchair. He said "Hello" right as Mrs. Williams stood over the rectangular coffee table and, hands clasped, said, "Izola, this is Paul, the young man I was telling you about. He lives all by himself across the street."

Izola turned to Paul and set her teacup on the coffee table. He stood and leaned over to shake her hand.

"Nice to meet you," he said, and thought, *I guess.* The problem with being Steady Paul, along with feeling like he was going to burst if he kept it up too long, was that sometimes women liked Steady Paul a little too much.

Her hand was soft and dry like the sides of Paul's mama's pin cushion. How did that pop into his head? How did he get so comfortable?

"I'm going to get you some tea, too," said Mrs. Williams, before shuffling back to the kitchen.

Paul looked at the dust that had collected on the old piano across the room. Mrs. Williams had called him over to try and set him up with this niece of hers. But this niece was fine enough that she shouldn't need any help. Was this as awkward for her as it was for him? He scoured his mind, thinking of an excuse to get back home. Something on the stove? Mrs. Williams knew he didn't cook much, which is why she gave him leftover meatloaf and mashed potatoes from time to time. Guest? Mrs. Williams had probably watched the door to his building like she usually did. Shower running? No. He was stuck.

"Live by your lonesome, huh?"

She had a nice voice, like her and Paul had already got past the "Where do you live/what do you like to do" nonsense. He could see her next to him at Winnie's Grill, rolling her eyes at the guys.

"Yeah, you?"

She nodded over her tea and held his eye for a second too long after he said, "Yeah." He said, "What?" when she didn't answer.

"I live on my own, too," she said. No invitation, just the same voice like a bottle full of laughs waiting to tip and roll out.

She looked to the kitchen door, then into her tea, and chuckled. Like that, he knew she'd read him. She'd seen through Steady Paul. The balloon popped, and he glanced at the front door before settling back into his seat.

Paul was nodding his own recognition when Mrs. Williams came back in. He stiffened his back when a wide tray with a single cup of tea appeared next to the left armrest. No matter what her niece saw, Mrs. Williams still got Steady Paul. Paul sloshed hot tea across his wrist when she asked, "You two getting it on?"

He moved the cup to his right hand and stuck the tea-stained one in his mouth, mind racing, wondering how to answer, then realized his mistake when Izola didn't miss a beat and said, "Yes, Auntie. We've got a lot to talk about, like how hard it can be to find the right," she paused, "roommate."

Paul looked up, burned hand still in his mouth. His eyes met Izola's and there was a beat. Were they gonna keep it together? No. Her shoulders started to shake until she had to set her teacup on the coffee table in front of her. He did the same and laughed, slapped his knee, and looked at old Mrs. Williams, who pretended to be in on the joke and smiled too.

It's a joke you can't tell because most folks don't

think it's funny. To have good news that wants to bust loose, but it's a tragedy to others. Food that makes your mouth sing, but when you try and serve it up, salted just right to make the flavor pop, no one wants a bite. That's what it's like.

4

Kevin

David met me in the lunch line, looking shifty. "You ready to do this?" I asked.

I put my tray on the metal runners and licked my lips at the hot dishes under the glass, the cookies and chips you can grab for yourself, and the milks resting on shiny ice.

Tyrell's five bucks turned into two bags of tater tots, a fruit cup, a cellophane pack of chocolate chip cookies, plus some raisin ones, a cheeseburger that David was gonna cut and I'd choose, a thing of strawberry milk, and two cans of Hawaiian Punch to drink after PE.

Our trays were piled high with food that looked delicious wrapped in greasy paper and golden crusts, and plastic that caught the up-high lights. When we passed loudmouth Tameka's table, she said something about "niggas in Ethiopia" to those project girls that she sits with.

Back in the corner past them was Tyrell, Leo,

and Spayne, sitting by the dookie-brown wall. Their table is ground zero for most of the flying food and noise that goes down during lunch. Tyrell's spot had a chocolate milk and his Braves hat. He stood over it with a sneaky smile, reaching over one of the project girls' shoulders, trying to grab an egg roll off her tray. She was smacking at his hand and yelling, "Boy stop!" but it sounded like she liked it. He did that stuff every day, even when he had his own lunch.

Me and David don't have our own table. We sat at an empty one near the food line with a white kid sitting alone at the other end. David cut the burger down the middle with a plastic knife and said, "Which one?"

I lifted the bun up to make sure that the cheese wasn't stuck over to one side and David looked shocked, and almost shouted, "Man, get your hands off the burger. I know you ain't wash them."

"I ain't had to share with you."

I grabbed the side closer to David and took a bite before setting it on my bag of tater tots. A big hand plunked down on the table between us. I looked up. Ashy, tea-colored fingers. Linty Starter jacket sleeve. Tyrell's terrier face.

He said, "I'll take this other piece," then grabbed David's side of the burger and bit off half, chewing all slow.

David jumped up so fast he knocked his knee on the bottom of the table. His tray jumped. He reached for Tyrell's elbow and yelled, "That's mine!"

Tyrell lifted the burger so his arm was cocked for a football pass and chewed with his mouth open to tease David.

"Not anymore," Tyrell chuckled, and pushed David away no problem.

Gray burger danced in his mouth, and his eyes were snake cold. David straddled his stool like he was giving birth to it.

"What the hell? Kevin!"

I realized I still had burger getting soft in my mouth. The same burger that Tyrell had half of. That I bought with Tyrell's money.

"Yeah, what the hell, Kevin?" Tyrell mimicked. "What are you two little faggots doing sitting next to each other with all this food, anyway?"

I heard a laugh, then another laugh at the next table. Tyrell rifled through the tray and spilled my tater tots, but I couldn't stand up because my legs had gone watery. His hand felt like it was messing up me, instead of my food.

I started feeling like jelly. Jelly that's weak. Jelly that filled me so I couldn't breathe. My eyes watered. I looked down to hide them, but then all I could see was my cookies disappearing into Tyrell's fist, and that was it. I shoved his hand away, and the fist full of cookies flew to the left, sinking into the only thing in the way—David's gut. The package burst, and cookie crumbs rained over the table. David gasped and doubled over, like in a movie when someone gets shot, and I felt lousy for making that happen. The lunchroom got real quiet.

Tyrell frowned at the empty cookie wrapper in his hand. Fury twisted David's face. He pushed himself up with his left hand on the table and brought back his right arm to punch. I heard someone behind me inhale so fast it whistled. David's wrist was further back than his elbow, like he was about to girl throw.

"No," I said, standing and leaning out over the table. My voice sounded choked. The front of my hoodie flopped into the tater tots.

If David hit Tyrell, there really would be a fight. We'd all get suspended, and me and Tyrell would never be cool. Tyrell finally figured out that the cookies were gone and brought his eyes up to me, then David, who drew his arm back further.

I told David, "It was me that did that. By mistake." I thought I'd sound cool like Luke Perry on *90210*, but my voice squeaked like I was about to be crying.

Then, David threw the punch. His arm was so skinny that his fist looked like a sucker on a stick, twisting, upside down, wrist-first, blocking out little bits of the people watching from behind us. Then, his fist made a last minute turn away from Tyrell and clocked my nose and upper lip. I was surprised before it hurt. Why the hell did he hit me?

ZERO FADE

Someone at the next table yelled, "Damn!"

My face got thick and hot from the blood rushing to where the punch landed. My eyes got teary, but I wasn't crying. The lunchroom lights turned into a thousand shimmery crystals. I shoved the tray at David as hard as possible, and pink strawberry milk splashed over the rest of the food. Tyrell stepped back across the aisle, palms out. Mr. Zipper the security guard ran up like a hornet in a sweaty polo shirt and grabbed David's shoulder with one hand, then pointed across the table at me.

"Let's go, fellas." He nodded at his old buddy, Tyrell, "You too."

"But I ain't—" Tyrell shook the crumbs inside the cookie wrapper.

"Save it for the office."

We left the lunchroom in a line, Mr. Zipper walking David and Tyrell, with me behind, tears falling from my eyes to the floor, sides of my head burning from people staring at me. Crying in school is like peeing yourself. It feels good to get it out, but you wind up with a bigger problem. I was in trouble, in a fight, deeper into it with Tyrell, and to top it all off, hadn't no one said nothing about my fade.

CHAPTER 4: TUESDAY

1

Kevin

Aisha's number is on page one forty-eight in the phone book. I say her number over and over in my head—320-2792—until it blurs—3202792—until I walk half a block, seeing her face in the light between the leaves, and come back in the middle—79232027, stopping at lucky seven and thinking, *That means I'm gonna have some good luck here.*

So far, just a little luck. She likes to talk about *The Simpsons*, even though she doesn't tape it and rewind it like I do. She probably talks on the phone and laughs at Bart, even though Homer is the funniest one. You only know that if you watch it close. But, that's cool. I could show her.

In class she sets her purple bookbag down and asks me questions that should be easy to answer.

"What you did this weekend, Kevin?"

My brain flashes memories: crumbling potato chips into a mug of vegetable beef soup, Mama blocking the TV with that spaceship-from-*Star Trek*-looking hat and yelling, "The deal was that, if you stay home from church, you do your GD homework, Kevin," looking out the window during Friday night TV ads and wondering if everyone else from school is at a party a block over fingering each other to Biggie Smalls songs. I can't tell Aisha none of that, so I say, "Oh, nothin'. You know."

The worst is the look she gives me when she realizes I'm not going to say nothing else. Then, I feel like someone in an old movie, running after a train.

Maybe I'll call her one night when Mama's in class and Laura's up the block doing whatever.

"Hey Aisha, this Kevin."

"Hey Kevin, what up?"

It's just her voice on the phone, fluty and wonderful, and I'll want to crack a joke and go, "Talking to you, what you thought?"

Don't want to offend Aisha, though. Get up all that nerve and have her hang up on me. Still, being wise might be the look. Don't tell no one that I read one of Laura's magazines, but, when I was looking for bra pictures, I saw that girls like guys with a sense of humor. It's true! Eddie Murphy gets nonstop booty. I've seen *Boomerang*. Telling Aisha I'm talking to her might work.

Making the call would have been a lot easier before yesterday, because that "mushy tushy" mess set me back, big-time. I'd have had better luck calling her last summer, before she even knew me.

2

I got to science lab early and sat at my usual table in the back. Aisha walked in less than a minute before the bell, eyes sleepy, looking forward. Other girls make an entrance, swinging their hips and looking at who's wearing what, but Aisha just walks one foot then the next. The way she didn't make an entrance was its own kind of entrance, and I appreciate that. It makes me the only one watching her, thinking *Sit next to me sit next to me* to hypnotize her. There was a little dirt on her Adidas windbreaker's stripes. The front of her orange hair was out of the ponytail and glowing around her head. She ain't sloppy, she just chill.

Does her jacket smell like onions again? What did she have for dinner? She put her hand on my shoulder.

"What up, Kevin."

I startled, moved my shoulder out so she'd touch it longer, said, "Good," then clapped my mouth shut because I'd said the wrong thing. To move on, I went, "How you?" and nodded once, smooth.

Aisha put her hand on her hip, shook her head, and laughed. Just like that, we had a moment. She threw her bookbag on the table across the aisle, and I was scheming on holding her hand. Then Demetric showed up.

Demetric's got big, caterpillar eyebrows he's always wiggling. This day, he was in a rugby shirt and some jeans that hung off just baggy enough. The bell rang, and Demetric hustled under Mr. Gordon's arm as he was closing the door. I put a hand on the table to hold my aisle seat and hoped Demetric sat to my right, far from Aisha.

No such luck. Smooth as butter across a pan, Demetric dropped his bookbag on the floor and hopped onto the stool next to Aisha, elbows on the table, staring at the blank chalkboard. Ugh.

Mr. Gordon's voice sounds like someone making fun of a boring teacher. It's impossible to pay attention to. I think he gave us an assignment as he walked through the room, leaving a two-inch wooden ball, a ruler, and a triangle-shaped, wood doorstopper on each table. I scooted over to join Aisha and Demetric. I can do that and not worry about her telling me to go back to my table.

I took the ruler and measured the doorstopper. Demetric rolled the ball back and forth on the table.

Aisha opened her notebook, and there was a big red heart drawn on the last page.

Demetric asked, "Who's that for, Aisha?"

I kept squinting at the wedge of wood we were supposed to measure.

"Oh, I dunno," Aisha said, shutting the cover.

"Like you drew a heart for no good reason. It's someone at school, ain't it?" Demetric was nodding at me. "Hear that, K.?"

"Yeah," I said, keeping my eyes on the table. "Aisha don't got a boyfriend though, right?"

Aisha had a pen with half a dozen buttons on top for different inks, and she was clicking out each color and pressing the tip to her thumb. I was clenching my thighs.

She said, "I dunno," again and cocked her head to the side. It was plain to see that she did like somebody.

I looked from my paper to her face, twice, wanting her to meet my eye and say, "I like Kevin," without even looking at Demetric and his rugby shirt.

"You like Kevin, Aisha?" Demetric asked, eyebrows up. My stomach hopped, then did a jackknife dive.

"Oh hell no," Aisha said, leaning back like we'd both done broccoli farts. "I'd even take you over Kevin, Demetric."

I threw my elbows on the table and knocked over the wedge. Mr. Gordon shouted, "How are those labs going, everybody?"

Demetric left one eyebrow up, rolled his neck back from Aisha, and said, "Go on."

"See, you might be a scrub, but at least you got a cute butt." Aisha was waving her pointer finger. "Kevin's got that mushy tushy."

With that, she poked my left buttcheek while it was squishing on my lab stool. I sat tall and flexed my cheeks. Couldn't believe she'd touched my butt. Didn't want it to happen like that, though. Demetric did a fake snicker and pumped his booty from the rung of his stool, hands on the table.

Aisha watched Demetric. I looked, too, because I had to see the difference between my ass and Demetric's. If girls were doing it, I needed to know what they were seeing. It looked like a butt. Thought mine did too.

We didn't finish the science lab.

3

For the rest of the day, I had to stop myself from touching my butt to make sure it wasn't poking out at people. After school, I hopped up my front steps and remembered Mama stopping on the stairs in Uncle Paul's building and saying, "Well, it's good for the gluteus maximus."

When I asked, "What's that," she said, "Booty

muscles," so loud it echoed up to the skylight.

Maybe if I walk up and down the stairs in my house a hundred times, my tushy won't be so mushy.

Inside, I made a plate of peanut butter and Chewy Chips Ahoys and opened the phone book on the table at the bottom of the stairs. Page one forty-eight has a greasy, red mark from some barbecue chip crumbs last week.

I stood at the table and used three fingers to jiggle my ass. Didn't feel too mushy to me. Aisha was probably trying to be funny. Doesn't make sense that she can say what she pleases while I clam up, but I'm glad I didn't come back with a "Like you should talk." That's the type of popping off at the mouth that got me grounded in the first place, and Laura's magazine said girls are concerned about their bodies. And, not getting any action is worse than being grounded, I can tell you that. Besides, Aisha's booty is round like two walnuts, and I'd be pleased to find out if it was mushy or not.

320-2792 is a quarter of the way down the first column of names. No address.

But, maybe Aisha hadn't been playing. For all I knew, she was sitting at home using the purple ink from that pen to draw science diagrams of my mushy tushy. Waddling around her living room with a couch cushion held over her butt, making her friends laugh by pretending to be me.

Or worse, maybe she never thinks of me at all. Maybe I'm a hundred percent invisible once I step out of science class. Maybe she'll be on my bus tomorrow, going to someone else's house while I'm three rows back, watching her hair glow marmaladey in the sun.

I squished another cookie with my tongue. Gravelly bits of peanut scraped the roof of my mouth. I rocked my thumbnail on the yellow phone book paper, drawing the left side of a heart.

4
Paul

Paul liked to drive out Brook Rd., where his grandfather used to drag race in the '40s. He'd heard that story five years back, on his grandpa's last Thanksgiving. Football was winding down on the TV and the old man said, "Seen that Ukrop's supermarket out Brook?"

"Sure," Paul answered, slouching on the couch and picking his teeth with a house key, ready for a boring conversation.

"Used to be a field. Hit 80 miles per hour one time driving past it, po-lice on my fender."

Paul lowered the key and said, "What?"

"We used to, you know," Grandpa hoisted an imaginary bottle of liquor, "get a brown bag and get to talking about whose car was faster. Next we knew, the girls were in the backseat, and we'd be out Brook Rd., swerving in the lanes, trying to nose ahead."

Grandpa had got smaller with age, like puckered lips. His green armchair was huge around him as he clutched an imaginary steering wheel.

"And the cops?" Paul asked.

"Oh, that was part of the fun. They'd see us and come out, lights flashing, but if we beat them to the county line, wasn't nothing they could do. They were city po-lice. We'd wave bye-bye and disappear."

Grandpa's hands opened and lifted off the invisible wheel.

The idea of disappearing stuck with Paul, and Brook Rd. became his place for thinking things over. He'd pretend like everything was black and white and all the cars were from the '40s.

Izola had called and said, "You gotta show me around. Thanks to my auntie, I know where the church and the Shoney's are at. Now, I know y'all country down here, but I got a feeling there's more to the city than just that."

Paul fought the urge to say, "Not much more," and picked her up with no real plan. When they passed the baseball diamond, he realized he was driving to his job, turned around in the bus station parking lot, and hit Brook Rd. They'd already reached the part where the median started, with trees growing out of brown mulch.

Izola said, "I coulda swore she asked if we were getting it on."

Paul was laughing so hard his forehead brushed the horn.

"Mmm, imagine that. She leaves the room for a minute and comes back to see us getting down on the couch."

They both hooted, and Paul hung his elbow out the window.

"She woulda spilled that tea everywhere. On the ceiling," he said.

"Thought it was you who did that."

She had him there. The "Welcome to Henrico County" sign was a stoplight away. When Grandpa died, pop had become the oldest, and Paul got bumped up a place in line, too.

"What's your pop like?" Paul asked, clicking on the turn signal and gliding into the left lane.

"Good man, but…" Izola trailed off. Paul kept his eyes on the road, letting her think. They passed over a manhole cover, worn smooth with age, and Paul pretended the car was Pac-Man eating one of those little video game pills.

"Everything is money with him. I'm in college, it's gotta be to get a better job. Never mind what I'm interested in."

"I take it he don't like fashion design too much," Paul said.

She laughed, looked out her window and bobbed her head to an imaginary beat.

"He doesn't think I'm gonna meet much of a man in my line of work."

"Well, you gotta look a bit harder, honey," said Paul, exaggerating the sass for the sake of the joke. "Not sure I'm the one."

They laughed then got quiet. Michael Jackson came on the radio and, as Paul was reaching to turn it up, Izola asked, "What's your pop like?"

He gave the volume the slightest bump and paused with his hand on the knob, imagining a red, brick wall. That's what his pop was like.

"We got some differences, too," he said slowly.

It was Izola's turn to nod and wait for Paul to keep going.

"He's not bad, but we ain't close."

Paul saw things with his father as being like string cheese. You let something out, pull off one little thread, and it connects to another bit of the cheese. So you pull that off too, and that sets loose another bit, which hangs off the side. So you get that too, and next you know, it's gone. No cheese. It's a bad feeling to know that the man who made you wouldn't understand the person you've been since birth.

"He don't know, huh?"

"Lord no. And I don't like the secrets. Having my guard up all the time? I don't want that. And you know, Kevin—"

"That's your nephew, right?"

"Mmm-hmm. Kevin don't know either. And last week, he told me I was like his pop and it got me thinking about my own pop—"

"You mean, like his pop like you *act* like his pop, or like his pop like you *is* his pop?"

"Like I is—*am* his pop."

They both smiled at the grammar. Paul always got a kick out of hearing Sheila correct the kids.

"And he don't know either, huh?"

"Nope. And if I don't tell him, will it be like some string cheese, too?"

"String cheese?"

"Nothin'," Paul replied. "You hungry?"

5

Kevin

I keep a *Victoria's Secret* catalog in my shirt drawer. It's from around Christmas, so the woman on the front is dressed like Santa, and there's a rectangle under her leg from where I ripped off the mailing label with Mama's name. I was looking for the catalog when I found my red Richmond Public Schools PE shirt, and it reminded me of that crazy red leather suit that Eddie Murphy wore in *Delirious*. I turned it inside out before putting it on, then shimmied my jeans to the floor and got some red sweatpants from the bottom drawer. They were too small, which made them tight on the thigh like Eddie Murphy's pants. I grabbed the *Delirious* tape from inside my desk, slapped it in the boombox, then strutted into the hallway to the sound of the man announcing the show.

As I walked into Mama's bedroom, the stage, I did a toothy Eddie Murphy grin and nodded across the unmade bed, feeling my pride rise as I took in the thousands of cheering fans. Full house tonight! The mirror on Mama's dresser starts at the waist, and hid the highwater part of my sweats, but I could feel a draft on my ankles. Mama won't use the heat in April.

I grabbed an oily hairbrush off the dresser, held it close to my chest like a microphone, and moved my lips to Eddie Murphy saying, "Thank you, thank you..."

I want to be Eddie Murphy, or be funny as him in my own way, and have someone to thank for something.

I paced the little strip between the bed and the dresser, still cheesing like Ed. The hairbrush smelled like Mama's shampoo. How could she ever have understood these jokes? My left hand hovered at my hip as I rubbed my thumb against the longer fingers.

"When I do my stand-up, I got rules..."

I wheeled left toward the door and passed the mic

to my left hand, looking in the mirror at my strut.

"Straight up, faggots aren't allowed to look at my ass when I'm on stage."

I covered my butt with my right arm and gave the crowd a minute to crack up. Aisha was sitting alone in the middle of the audience, by Mama's plaid comforter. Her pop had dropped her off, and she was caught in a trance watching me. I turned back, tossed the mic over to my right hand, and walked toward the window, windmilling my left hand as if to say, "There's more coming."

"That's why I keep moving while I'm up here."

The crowd laughed again. I was ten feet tall. I was Eddie Murphy on that stage. Then, Mama's voice broke in.

"Hey, Beverly Hills Cop!"

I stopped and dropped the hairbrush to my side. Ice crept up my legs. The tape played on, Eddie Murphy saying, "I know when you're looking there, too, because my ass gets hot."

Suddenly, the PE shirt and riding-up sweatpants felt stupid. In the mirror, I wasn't Eddie Murphy anymore. I was some seventh grader who couldn't do nothing but get grounded and play around with his mama's hairbrush.

"Hey Mama."

She stood in the doorway, tilting her head. I put my eyes down and tried to squeeze through the little space she left. *Make this not happen.*

She stood still. I felt like I'd been caught in the neighbor's yard.

"Hey yourself," she said.

I walked backwards as she came into the room, nodding her head and looking around.

Eddie Murphy said, "I have this nightmare that I go to Hollywood and find out that Mr. T is a faggot," and the crowd laughed in my bedroom.

"Eddie Murphy, huh?" she smiled and frowned, still not sure what was going on. I got ready to point out her copy of the same tape, right there on the dresser, if she fronted on the cussing.

"Yeah. Eddie Murphy." I looked her in the eye and put the hairbrush back, sneaky as possible.

"Don't you have some homework to be doing, that's due in less than, um, *forty-eight hours*?"

The audience on the tape laughed, synching right up with Mama's dumb joke about the Eddie Murphy movie. I wanted to be back in my room, closer to the boombox, having a good time.

"Alright, I'll do it." I went for the door again.

"OK then. Why are you wearing your gym clothes?"

I stopped with my back to her and really wanted to pick a wedgie. Then she said, "And those old pants that don't fit? I thought I got rid of those pants."

"I'll change before I do my homework."

Mama was probably mad at having more laundry

to do.

"Yes you will. But you didn't say why you had those clothes on."

She could take the fun out of anything.

"I just, uh…" She was looking at me with her chin up. She liked Eddie Murphy, but she'd never understand trying to dress like him. In science lab, the fastest way from A to B is a straight line. Same in a conversation. No sense in lying. Real quick, I said, "I was trying to dress like he did in *Delirious*."

Mama looked me head to toe with her lips pursed and a shine in her eye. A laugh slipped out as she said, "So you're Eddie Murphy now."

I waited for her to say I'd never look like Eddie Murphy, because then I could tell her that it didn't matter what Eddie Murphy looked like, what mattered was how funny he was. That wouldn't cause more trouble. But Mama just kicked her shoes off at the foot of the bed, walked out and crossed to the bathroom. I hurried to my bedroom, turned off the boombox and changed, leaving the sweatpants and t-shirt on the floor. The tub was running, and I heard Mama clomping downstairs to get one of her beers. Even if Aisha said I had a mushy tushy, and I knew I'd never look like Eddie Murphy, I'd get my own thing going somehow.

I was stacking schoolbooks on my desk when Mama called, "Kevin, come in here a minute." Her voice echoed off the water in the tub, and she sounded far off. I opened the bathroom door to find Mama in her usual position—sideways on the closed toilet with her back against the wall, holding a beer can. Her navy blue slacks were rolled up, and she was wiggling her toes in the tub's hot water. The cool air from the hall fogged her glasses, and she tipped her head, so they slid down her nose.

"Eddie Murphy, huh?"

She burped into the top of her fist, then set the beer on the back of the toilet by the air spray.

"Mama, I got homework to do."

"You've had homework to do. It can wait two more minutes while you talk to me. So, you like that Eddie Murphy tape?"

She sloshed her feet and made a creepy, happy face at the rippling water.

"Yeah, yeah," I said.

"Why?"

"Because he funny!"

What did she think? The bathroom was hot, and my upper lip got sweaty.

"Well, what *is* so funny?"

"Just, like, the way he tells some of those jokes.

And how you know that being a funny dude kept him out of trouble sometimes."

Staying outta trouble. She'd like that. I squished my butt against the doorframe and picked at the chipped paint, waiting to escape.

"Yeah? What about all the things he says about, um, gay guys?"

Mama pulled the beer off the back of the toilet and took a sip, squinting at me over the can. She hates the word "faggot." Once, Laura called Michael Jackson that, and Mama got serious and said it was gay people's version of "nigger," and there was no reason to use it. That sat funny with me, because being black's not nasty like getting naked with dudes is.

"Those jokes are good too. All his jokes are funny, Mama."

She shook her head and sighed. The water splashed.

"But don't you think it's messed up that he makes fun of, um, gay guys? Do you think that's fair?"

"Sure. I mean, he makes fun of everybody, right? Like that joke about Mr. T. I mean, we know Mr. T's not really gay."

"Do we? I guess, but," she leaned her head back to finish off the beer, "he seems really scared of fa—gay guys."

"Yeah, that is weird. Who'd be scared of a gay guy?"

Everyone knows they fight all slappy like girls.

"Exactly," Mama said.

The fog was gone from her glasses, and she looked straight at me. Finally we were agreeing about something. I was starting to feel crazy, like I really wanted to do homework, and moved to head out.

"Do you ever play that tape for your Uncle Paul?"

"No. He listens to the radio in his car and stuff."

That "Between the Sheets" song from the barbershop popped into my head, and I felt real weird about being in the bathroom with Mama. Why was she asking about Uncle Paul? Did she know about Xavier the barber? My fade wasn't gay, was it?

"OK, I see," she said.

"Why? Does Uncle Paul like Eddie Murphy?"

She kicked the water again.

"I don't know, baby. He might. Me and my baby brother don't always like the same things, even though sometimes I'm surprised at how much of the same stuff we do like."

She must have got drunk off that beer.

"Uh, right. Say, I think the barber Uncle Paul took me to was a ... gay guy."

"Yeah? Why you think that?"

She put the empty beer back on the toilet, then settled with her elbow resting on the toilet paper holder. The water gurgled as she moved her feet.

"He just seemed gay," I said, making my wrists go

loose and wiggling my butt.

"Well, so did you just now."

"Shut up, you know what I mean."

"Don't tell me to shut up. And hey, even so, that gay barber gave you a nice haircut, didn't he? Better than your mama can do."

She looked down into the water. I got guilty for a second and ran my hand up the back of my head. Sharp bits of stubble were already coming in. I wished my cut would last a couple more weeks. Then what? Try and get grounded again so Uncle Paul could take me back to that barber? It's one thing to go there by accident, but going back…uh-uh. I shivered, remembering Xavier's fingers tickling the side of my head, and said, "Yeah, but you know, it was still weird."

"You got to remember, Kevin. What that barber does at home is for him to worry about. When he's at work, he's professional as can be." She pointed at my head.

"Yeah, you're right," I said, but didn't mean it. I just wanted out of that bathroom. Maybe Uncle Paul knew another barber.

"OK now," Mama said. "You start in on that homework."

I turned to the door and said, "Mmm-hmm," then stopped when Mama said, "By the way. I'm goin' on a date Friday."

A date?! I turned and hooked my thumbs on my jeans' front pockets.

"A date."

"Yes," she said, raising her eyebrows, daring me to be surprised.

I was surprised. I was also mad and jealous because she had a date and I didn't. I got a lump in my throat, and my thighs tingled, like when I heard about people my age getting it on, or the time Onaje Turner was on the news because his grandma's house burned down.

"With who?"

"A man from work. You remember Earnest, from the church?"

Earnest is froggy and wiry. Little man with a mop who always seems like he has his arms around a flock of jokes waiting to fly out.

"Him?" Was he gonna bring the dang mop on the date?

"Yeah, him. Friday night."

"What am I supposed to do?" I started getting loud.

I'll never tell her this, but sometimes not having nothing to do on a Friday night is cool because Mama joins me at the TV with a bowl of ice cream and jokes on the shows like, "No way could a family of seven keep a house that clean," and, "Too sassy. They'd get a slap for that 'round here, huh?"

That wasn't happening this Friday. She was gonna be slow dancing in the church aisle with moonlight glittering through the stained glass and a mop leaned on one of the pews.

"You stay in. You are grounded, you know."

Mama wouldn't always be on that toilet seat, talking to me. She wouldn't always be in the kitchen, trying to un-burn Laura's cooking. And now she had a date, and I never had a date, so screw that. And screw my pops for never coming back, even though I wrote him a letter with just his name and no address on the envelope and dropped it in the mailbox—just to try— last year. And screw this Earnest, who probably didn't have a car and rode his mop like a witch broom. What do old people do on dates anyway? Wasn't no one gonna feel up Mama in a movie theater! I broke out to my room and sat on the far end of the bed, looking out the window.

A minute later, Mama knocked. I didn't say nothing. She swung the door open.

"Kevin, baby."

I still didn't say nothing.

"You know how you like to go out? I do too," she said.

I twisted around and said, "But you do go out all the time." I wanted to push the bed at her.

"I—Where?"

"You goin' to work. Then you goin' to school. And

you ain't never here."

My voice hiccupped at the end because I was crying. Screw crying and her stupid nursing school.

"That's different, and you know it. That ain't goin' out, goin' out. That'd be like you goin' to school and saying it was some social—"

"Stay in," I said, like begging. "Stay in," like an order.

Mama opened her mouth, and her tongue turned to a fork. I thought I was going to get it all over again, but then the door creaked open downstairs, and Laura's keys jingled onto the phone table. Had I shut the phonebook?

Footsteps came up, and Mama leaned over the rail with her butt pointed out. Did Earnest look at that at work? Did he like that? Nasty! Mama asked, "Where you been?"

"Out," Laura said.

Footsteps kept going. Mama said, "Yeah, no kiddin'."

Laura walked past the bathroom and disappeared on the other side of my doorway. I scooted across the bed so I could kick into my homework. Only time I wanna do homework is when Mama's talking at me. She turned from the banister.

Laura said, "I was out, and now I need to do my homework."

I guess it's the same for Laura.

"Who are these new friends? I know you're not out with Sharese, right?"

Laura was quiet for a second.

"No. Not Sharese."

That was the first time since Thanksgiving that I heard Laura say Sharese's name, instead of "Ho" or "Trick."

"Then who?"

Mama talked to Laura different than me. More patient, like they really were friends. It sounded fake when she tried to talk like that with me, and that was fine because me and Mama aren't friends. I'm a man who does man things that she can't understand.

I listened because I wanted to know who Laura was kicking it with, too. Laura's life had become a mystery real fast, while me and David were watching *The Simpsons*, and she was "out" doing something. Laura stepped back into view. She looked worn out.

"Tracy," Laura answered.

"Tracy?"

"Yeah. She go to John Marshall, too. We in math class."

"Oh."

Laura started to turn to her room.

"Laura, I should tell you while I got you here," Mama said. "I'm going on a date Friday."

There was a second of silence. My bedsprings creaked when I clenched my fists and thighs at "date."

Then, Laura busted out laughing. Her head was the only thing that moved, and it was shaking around scary, letting out big "Ha's" while her hands stayed at her sides, flying frog fingers spread.

Mama was quiet. Laura bent forward and slapped her knee, then stood up, loose, one eyebrow up.

"You going on a date?"

She grinned so big that her cheeks touched her eyelids. There was something different about her, like she was only looking out the bottom of her eyes.

Mama said, "Laura. Are you high?"

What?

Laura stood straight, popped her eyes open, "No."

"You look high," Mama said.

Got the getting it on/Onaje on the news feeling again. Laura couldn't be on drugs. I yelled, "How you know what high look like?"

Still staring Laura down, Mama reached her right hand out, fingers spread wide to hush me. In my brain was Mama in the Dr. Dre video with the cookout, smoking a blunt.

"I ain't high," said Laura, shrugging and looking to the bathroom, then past me in my room. She sniffed her upper lip.

"You look high. And you actin' high. Laughin' at me like that. This Tracy get high?"

Laura's mouth opened and snapped shut with a hollow pop. She said, "No."

ZERO FADE

"Come here."

Laura paused, then took three steps across the hall. Mama grabbed the collar of Laura's jean jacket and sniffed it like she did diapers on the babies at her work.

"You smell like cigarettes."

Laura pulled away and said, "Tracy mama smoke."

"You smelled like them before. And it's *Tracy'sss… mama… sssmokesss*."

They were staring each other down. I went, "Ooh!" and Mama said, "Cool it, Kevin."

"I'm not high," Laura stalked into her room. Mama looked at her closed door. My stomach felt twisty like when I got a bad grade. Was Laura on drugs? Was she gonna get a nest of crackhead hair on her head? Steal my boombox and trade it to a dealer?

"Mama, how come Laura ain't got grounded?"

Mama walked to my doorway.

"How come Laura *did not get* grounded?"

She paused, then leaned back out into the hall and said, good and loud, "Only reason Lil' Ms. Attitude didn't get grounded was because I can't have both of y'all moping around the house at the same time. Might mess up my blood pressure."

Quiet from Laura's room.

Mama said, "She'll get what's coming when it gets there," then went in her room and shut her door too.

Her Patti LaBelle tape came on, and I knew she was laying on her bed with her arms and legs stretched toward each corner like she was in medieval times, about to be drawn and quartered. She'd do that for a while with her eyes shut, then get up and make dinner. I picked up a pencil and shot rays out of its tip at the wall, where I pictured Earnest's froggy face.

At seven, my homework was done, and I knocked on Mama's door. That woke her up. When I asked about dinner, she rubbed her head, and I got a good feeling like we'd be getting to eat out. After she hit the bathroom, she said, "Laura, Kevin, I'm taking you downtown!" which is her joke because she drives an old police cruiser and likes to pretend we're under arrest when she's driving us places.

Laura shuffled into the hall, and I asked, "Where we going, Mama?"

Mama had half a smile and wouldn't answer.

When Mama got the car, Uncle Paul bought her a police hat, and she'd wear it when she was driving. It was mad embarrassing, so I got in the habit of ducking down in the back seat. She hadn't worn the hat in a while, but I still ducked down.

Whenever we drive at night, the cars near us think we're undercovers, so they slow down and let Mama past, shooting us looks from the corners of their eyes. It was cool to zip past people, but it also

ZERO FADE

sucked because we aren't no Rodney King beaters, and I didn't want someone to think I was. The car was quiet, just a humming noise, Laura looking out the passenger side window. We pulled into the Burger King on Brook Rd. The neon lights in the restaurant left streaks of shadow on our faces, and Laura ate her fries so fast she was pushing them around the wax paper burger wrapper trying to pick them up. Mama sipped her soda and counted the change in her lap, then bought three cherry pies.

CHAPTER 5: WEDNESDAY

1

Kevin

Laura's old boyfriend Corey used to drop me off at middle school on the way to the high school. One morning in October, we stopped so Laura could run into the store. It felt realer without Laura in the car, just me and Corey kicking it for a minute. He was slim and light-skinned with one of those pointy chins just made for a goatee. He was a little taller than me and wore his clothes baggy, and I was trying to work up the nerve to ask him for some of his old clothes when him and Laura broke up. I knew he would have said yes, because he was always slipping me things.

On this day, he leaned over the driver's seat and handed me one of those old tapes with bumpy, tan plastic on the back of the case. The guy on the cover was smiling in a red suit and just had a name. Eddie Murphy. No MC, no DJ nothing, just *Eddie Murphy, Delirious*.

Guess I frowned, because Corey said, "That's some comedy."

He was always cool. Looked me in the eye like what I thought mattered. Past Corey were the neon green and orange cigarette posters under the store's chicken wire windows. I didn't wanna be late, but busting in at the bell like I wasn't some goody-goody would be alright. Why was he handing me this old tape? I'd seen ads for Eddie Murphy movies. They looked corny.

"One thing, Big Man," Corey said. "Play this one quiet at home." He rocked his neck left, stretching it, then turned to face front. His eyes appeared in the rearview mirror, "You don't want your mama hearing the cursing."

Corey was super respectful to Mama. When he rang the bell, his powder blue North Carolina hat would be in his hands by the time she opened the door. He called her "Ms. Phifer," too.

Except for "faggot," or if I was cursing at her, language wasn't a big deal to Mama. Before she has her beer after work, she stands at the phone table, passing each bill from one hand to the other, going, "BS ... BS ... BS ..."

But, I didn't want to tick Corey off, so the first time I played that Eddie Murphy tape was real low while Mama was downstairs cooking. I was looking forward to checking it out, but I didn't understand why he was passing me some old tape. No one at school had heard of this.

Good thing I had my door shut, because right off, Eddie Murphy had me doing one of those laughs where I knew I had to be quiet, and that just made it harder to stop, so I was doubled over my desk, tears tapping on my homework. It wasn't what Eddie Murphy said, but how he said it, like he was just a dude who had lived these things and thought about them until they got really funny. What about my life would be funny later? Not getting any? No cable?

I got real into that tape and would listen on my Walkman in bed, laughing into my blanket. Eddie Murphy's voice had me bouncing on my feet at school, not always saying words, just making a warm, humorous sound. I had *Delirious* memorized within two weeks and set it aside, playing it in my head. While I was putting on my pants in the morning, I'd hear Eddie Murphy as Mr. T barking, "You look mighty cute in them jeans boy." It was my thing. A magic fossil I'd dug up.

One night, Mama was propped up on her bed looking like a bossy queen with all her pillows, checking over my Language Arts homework. The wood lamp on the nightstand made the homework glow gold.

I remember burping and tasting the garlic bread we'd had with our spaghetti right before I spotted a copy of *Delirious* in the tape case on Mama's dresser.

Mama likes boring stuff like Luther Vandross, and she gets down by dancing around the hall in her sweatpants to "New Attitude," so I never check out her tapes. That's why I was thrown to see Ed in there by a Phyllis Hyman tape. Hymen. Nasty.

My homework blocked Mama's face. Had she found the tape and taken it? Corey was gonna hate me. Why hadn't Mama said nothing yet? I rocked foot to foot. The paper came down. Mama said, "'Clamber' isn't a fisherman, Kevin."

"You sure?"

Would she hurry up? I wanted to finish the cookies 'n' cream ice cream in front of *Hangin' with Mr. Cooper*, and it started in three-and-a-half minutes. Was she gonna say anything about the tape?

"Yes, I'm sure. That's why I said it. Look that one up in your dictionary, then come back and tell me."

"Are the other ones right?"

She held out the paper.

"You need to check over your work, and stop wasting my time."

I snatched the homework. Wasting time? She had all the time in the world to boss me around.

I opened two desk drawers at once so it wouldn't sound like I was playing. I pulled my dictionary from the top drawer, then eased it shut. In the next drawer down, by a glittery second grade art project, was Corey's Eddie Murphy tape, with a chip missing from the top-right corner of the case.

So Mama had her own copy of *Delirious*.

There were pictures of Mama with big glasses and afro sheen from around when *Delirious* came out. Even though Mama liked to say, "I used to get down too," when Laura would act embarrassed by her, it was impossible to imagine that Mama had ever clapped her hands in a group of people dancing, passed a joint with her friends, or listened to something as wild as Eddie Murphy. You'd think that if she'd ever been into that, she'd be cooler. That she wouldn't dish out punishments, because she knew how much it sucked to stay in. But there was that tape—proof that Mama used to be cool.

I found "Clamber" in the dictionary. *Hangin' with Mr. Cooper* was a rerun. Ice cream was good, though.

2

David got a day of in-school suspension for punching me in the lunchroom. Me and Tyrell just got written up, which didn't mean nothing but that they'd call home if I got written up again.

Assistant Principal Singer is this small, churchy-looking man with big glasses and a gray suit. He blinked slow across his desk like we'd woke him up from a nap, then signed our write-up sheets and looked at me extra-long because I'd never been in his office before. "You two are dismissed."

If that's how easy getting sent to the office is, then I won't get so bent outta shape next time. I was worried about what was happening to David in there, but it was cool to be walking with Tyrell. Out in the hall, I put a hand up for five, but he was already walking away. He stopped and screwfaced me until I dropped my hand. Then he said, "Nigga, that's your boy in there. Don't go trying to dap me. You sellin' him out."

He shook his head and turned away. I felt low and wished I had my lunch, but only the parts I would have got with my own money.

I should have been in the office, too. But why did David punch me? What if he was sitting across from the assistant principal, hanging his head and saying, "It all happened because...," then, pausing and sniffling like he was on Court TV, "Kevin stole money from Tyrell, and Tyrell just came to get it back!"

If he caved in the office, I'd be pissed at him, in trouble with the principal, and in even deeper with Tyrell. And I'd have nowhere to go. I'd be one of those kids who sat alone at lunch.

It never happened, though. David wasn't on the

bus after school, and the office hadn't left a message at my house. I should have been happy, but the silence was worse than being yelled at or punched. It hung over my head and spun my stomach, and I couldn't sneak over to David's before Mama got back from work because he musta been mad at me, and I didn't feel like looking at Aisha's number because my tushy was probably still mushy, so I cut on the TV but couldn't focus. *Judge Judy*? Uh-uh.

David was at the bus stop on Wednesday morning with hard balls of fist in his jacket pockets as he paced under the tree, kicking at the dead grass. He didn't look like he'd turned into a thug during in-school, but my stomach still dropped, and I burped and tasted sour milk. I shouldn't have had OJ with my cereal. How mad was David at me? Had he told? Was I in trouble at school? Why did he punch me? Why did I cry in school, or ever?

When I got closer, David peeked up, then quickly down, and went back to pacing and kicking up ankle-high clouds of dirt. I stopped just shy of him and looked up the street for the bus. David stopped with his back to me and dug in the dirt with his toe. I had to say something.

"Don't mess up those sneakers, man."

The toe stopped moving. I inched back and asked, "So, what happened?"

David's shoulders and bookbag drooped. I started to say something else, but he spun and leaned his face into mine. There was crust in the corners of his mouth.

"I got in-school, man. You know that by now."

He said "in-school" like someone might say "head lice," or "moving to Chicken Switch, Missouri."

"Yeah, yeah. What was that like?"

I pictured in-school as a class of thugs, the teacher standing behind her desk with a M16. David came in closer, "Man, it sucked! You know when you wanna get out of class? Well, imagine if class went on *all day*." He slapped my chest twice for emphasis.

"I just did homework. And sat there. And someone brought me my new homework. And I did that. And then—"

"Did the assistant principal ask about me at all?"

David started shouting and the birds stopped chirping. "No he did not ask about you."

On a porch up the block, an old lady in a yellow and green housecoat stopped shaking the dust from a rug and stared at us. The sun reflecting off her glasses made her eyes look like huge fingernails.

I stepped back saying, "OK, fine," and feeling tiny for being scared of David.

I should have been relieved, but I felt worse. How could I get David to stop being mad at me? I was mad back. Mad at David for being mad at me and for punching me.

"Kevin, it ain't always about you. Hell, I don't know why I kept my mouth shut. This is all your fault." A seed of spit hit my cheek. "If you hadn'ta stole that five, I never would have been in in-school and—"

"You grounded?"

"No."

Ms. Gunderson didn't run a tight ship like that. David kept going, voice coming from his stomach and getting louder, shaking his open hands on either side of his face, "But I got in-school."

He was really up on me. And he hadn't brushed his teeth that morning.

"Nigga, you punched me." My body jerked, and I almost kissed David. Foul.

"Yeah, yeah I did." David stepped back into the tree's shade, nodding and looking around him.

"How you gonna do that?" I asked.

David and his morning breath busted back at me, "Did you forget? You punched me first... Nigga."

"But that was a accident. Look, man, look..."

I wasn't sure where to go. David cocked his head and stared at me.

"... I owe you one."

"Owe me one? Owe me one what? One day of in-school?"

"I just owe you one. Thank you."

ZERO FADE

It was weird to be saying formal stuff like "thank you" to my best friend. Friends don't have to do that because they already know it's out there. I bet Tyrell never says "thank you" to Spayne.

But it worked. David settled back on his heels, and a breeze rustled the new leaves over us. Beyond David's head, I saw the bus coming around the corner. David cocked his ear, then nodded and said, "Yeah, man. Yeah..." then rolled his lips back into a crazy grin and waggled his shoulders. I flinched, then he said, "Sssssssmokin'!" in a goofy, deep voice.

The bus was rolling through the stop sign. I stopped being mad and just got confused. What had he been learning in in-school?

"Smoke what?"

The bus doors hissed open. David ran up the steps, turned his back to the driver and shouted, "Sssssssmokin'!" down at me. The church girls in the front rows got quiet. I walked tall past them, bad because my best friend had in-school. Me and David took seats in the middle. The back is for eighth graders.

"What the hell is wrong with you, David? You're acting corny as hell," I asked across the aisle, trying to hide how funny I thought he was.

The bus took off toward the park.

"Kevin! It's *The Mask*. New Jim Carrey movie!"

"Word?"

David made buckteeth and mocked me, saying, "Word?" in a dumb, high voice.

Jim Carrey was my favorite comedian until I got that Eddie Murphy tape. His show, *In Living Color*, was one of the first things I watched on TV that wasn't some wimp nonsense like Urkel. One of the worst things was when they started showing *In Living Color* half an hour later, and Mama wouldn't let me sit up and watch it, but Laura could. That was super unfair, and Laura would torture me by trying to tell me about what I'd missed. Her impression of Fire Marshall Bill, pretending to stab herself with a cereal spoon, couldn't even touch the real thing, and sometimes she'd even mix up the different Wayans brothers. She didn't deserve to stay up and watch it.

And now Jim Carrey had a new movie out. The bus rolled past Tyrell's stop. He'd missed again.

"Yeah, Kevin. There was an ad for it on last night. I taped it."

"What's the deal?"

"He plays a nerd who gets an African mask and turns into this crazy, green guy."

Bert from *Sesame Street* is a yellow guy, and he ain't funny, but knowing it was Jim Carrey gave it some potential.

"You still got that tape?"

"Of course, man!"

The floor around the Gunderson's TV stand is

covered with stacks of VHS tapes that David fills with shows. Every time I go over there, David has something new to show me.

My side of the couch is by the apartment door. David's is by the windows and Ms. Gunderson's pillow with the picture of her at the state fair. David would get on his knees like he was praying to the TV and start going through the black plastic videotapes. The writing on the labels was usually wrong, because David was always taping over things. *Cooley High* would actually have three episodes of *The Simpsons*, the party scene from *Cooley High*, then a rerun of *In Living Color* with commercials from the summer. David would put the right tape in the VCR and get on the couch with the remote pointed out, ready to hit Fast Forward and turn the screen into squiggles.

3

By the end of school, I was going, "Sssmokin'," too, not caring that girls were raising their eyebrows like I was wack. I had to go to David's to see the ad. When we got off the bus, we took the long way around the block to avoid my house, crossing the side street and walking through the pointy shadow of the steeple from the corner church. It felt good to be walking with him. That's the cool thing about friends. You can forget when something goes wrong.

"You talk to Aisha in science class today?" David asked.

We don't talk about girls a whole lot. There's not much to talk about. But I'd brought up her name, and he knew I was into her.

"Yeah, for a second. In the hall."

I hadn't told David about "mushy tushy," though. I'm gonna be the first of us to get a girl, so David can't know Aisha said that. No one can.

"Cool," David looked at the sidewalk. He never talked about girls, except for once, when he said Sandra from grade school was "fine," and his voice sounded like a guy on TV. I'd laughed, and David just stood there, not sure what to do next. I hadn't heard about Sandra since, but David had a point—her chest had filled out over the summer, and they balanced out the chicken pox scars on her face. We walked past a four-flat with an open window bumping some music. I tried to catch the beat and walk like those guys who've got the funkiest songs in their head.

Right when I was hoping he'd drop the subject, David asked, "Think you're gonna ask out Aisha?"

Why'd she have to go and say that "mushy tushy" mess to Demetric? I still liked her though, and it was more than just a checking-out-a-low-cut-shirt-across-the-room type of thing. She actually talked to me. I can't just turn that off.

"I might, man. I might."

"What are you gonna ask her to do?"

"All I said was 'I might.' I need to think about it some more."

That hung in the air. What would me and Aisha do? Make out in a movie. Go to the food court and get ice cream. Get chicken then ice cream. Hold hands and feel her greasy chicken fingers. Put my arm around her. I'd like to ask her out and just spend a day with my arm around her, all warm, but with extra deodorant on so my pits won't be sweaty.

Then, David said, "Girls like doing different things than we do. You should ask her if she wants to go to the mall or something. Girls love walking around the mall."

He put his hands on his backpack straps.

"How do you know, David? With your virgin ass."

"Oh, and you ain't!"

He had me there. I kicked a wet newspaper in a plastic bag and didn't say nothing.

"All I'm saying is, if you take a girl out, it can't just be about you," he said.

I hate when David's right. Man. He'd probably go on a date and do whatever girls like to do, like go in the underwear section of the department store, or get their nails done. I laughed. David would get Mickey Mouse airbrushed on his nails.

"What?" he asked.

"Nothing."

We turned onto North Ave., where the store and the Chinese restaurant are and you can't walk like a guy who's never kissed nobody and is scared to ask out some girl from science class. You've gotta move like you own the sidewalk, like if someone said something about science class, you'd go, "Science what?" and laugh into your fist.

As we passed the laundromat, I put a bounce in my stride and let my arms go loose.

"You're walking crazy, Kevin."

"What you talking about?"

David dropped his hands from his backpack straps and shimmied his shoulders, doing an exaggerated gangster bop. He looked hilarious, but I wasn't going to let that on.

"The hell is that?"

"You know you're doing it, Kevin."

"Sssmokin'!"

We cut into David's alley. Since his place backs onto a busier street, the alley is paved, with big garbage cans and dark oil stains.

There ain't much to our neighborhood. Houses with little yards. Old people houses with long-grass yards. Four-flats with dead yards. Pitbulls clanging fences. Yellow grass. Orange Cheetos bags. Green glass bottles. So, I like walking down a different alley or going around the park and coming in from the other side. It makes the neighborhood feel new. Sometimes, I wish I could move somewhere with new girls and no Tyrell, but this is the only place I know, so I don't want to leave either.

Speaking of Tyrell, I jumped a mile when the plastic-tipped butt of a Black 'n' Mild cigar hit the ground at my feet, splashing sparks across my sneakers.

Husky-voice Tyrell shouted, "Heads up, bitches!"

David hightailed it to duck behind a dumpster, and I looked up. Tyrell was on a third-story fire escape, with a huge, white shirt draped on his head like a Middle Eastern king. His belly was a Slinky hanging over the front of his jean shorts.

I shouted, "Come on, man. You almost messed up my sneakers!" and swept my hand over the toe of my shoe, hoping that, from up there, Tyrell couldn't tell that these were the same black British Knights I've had since back to school.

"Whatever. I'm trying to burn them clean!"

David was peeking around the dumpster. The little cigar's sweet, old man smell drifted up from the ground.

"How's your sister, anyway?" Tyrell asked, leaning a forearm on the railing and looking down from inside the shadow of his shirt.

"My sister?"

What the hell did he want with Laura?

"Yeah, your sister."

Maybe getting written up together made him like me.

"She fine."

"Damn right she is!"

He laughed more and shook the railing. Man am I sick of being laughed at. I picked up the cigar by its damp tip and overhanded it up at Tyrell, sending it flipping like a boomerang past the z-shaped fire escape. Tyrell frowned so hard I thought fire would shoot out his nose. David made a noise like a question mark.

The cigar bumped off the railing to the left of Tyrell, sparked, and fell straight down like a shot bird. Tyrell watched it, puckering his lips like he still wanted to smoke, then yelled, "You little bitch!" when it dropped dead to the ground. He bolted for the fire escape. The white shirt flew off of his head and puffed like a ghost in the air. His belly jiggled as he hit the first stair, and for half a second, I thought about standing my ground to prove I wasn't a punk sellout, but then I heard the scrape of David's feet, and turned to see my best friend's bookbag bouncing as he took off down the alley, so I hit a runner's crouch and ran for my life, too.

David ran clear past his own back door, and turned the corner. Three steps in, and I was breathing heavy with a whistling in my throat, imagining Tyrell as a slobbering wolf chasing us through the desert.

Streaking down the block, me and David's feet were locked in stride, sounding heavier each time they landed. I scrambled up the front steps of David's building and held out my arms to keep from hitting him while he fumbled with his keys. My palms hit the bricks to the right of the door. My fingers were still sticky from the spit on Tyrell's cigar. Nasty. I wiped my hands on the butt of my jeans and looked back. The block was empty, a western movie before the big shootout. Not even the flutter of an old lady's curtain. David pushed the door open and ran in. I caught the door and walked, panting. Sweat popped out on my pits, stomach, and face.

It was musty in the apartment building hall, and I felt alive. Blood rushing, breath quick. Funny how much trouble you can get in when you're already grounded.

David already had his apartment door closed, and I had to knock.

"You alone?" he asked through the door.

"Yes, loser." I leaned on the doorframe. My thighs were singing from the run.

The door opened a crack, and David peeked over the chain, then shut the door to unlatch it. I was thirsty but didn't want to go anywhere near David's windows in case Tyrell was down there again. I sank into the familiar couch, feeling my shoulders loosen up.

David pushed a tape into the VCR and strutted

around the coffee table in the silly, gangster stroll he'd been doing earlier. Jim Carrey whirled to life on the screen, even funnier than David's impersonation.

"Rewind it," I said.

David already had his finger on the button. This was going to be our joke for a while. Didn't no one else at school know about *The Mask*. Things were looking up.

4

I was trying to do homework at my desk when funk started bumping from Mama's room. Pistol crack snares and a strutting bassline. The rhythm found me, and I bobbed my head. Laura was cheering, "Aww, Mama!" through the wall. Too thin wall. Can't let the mattress squeak when I'm jerking off before sleep.

They'd been doing some girl stuff, going through clothes, and every now and then, some laughter would flutter out into the hall. It was wack that Mama said tapes during homework were "too distracting," but here she goes having fun. I felt kinda jealous, so I went over there.

That was a big mistake. Shiny disco shirts were thrown across Mama's bed, with jewelry boxes open like deep-sea treasure chests. The tape was cranked until it fuzzed out, and the whole sloppy place had an electric shock feel. Laura stood by the bed grinning and clapping to the rhythm, but that wasn't nothing, because Mama was on my Eddie Murphy stage with her back to the door, bobbing her head side-to-side and dropping her spine every two beats, bopping her butt left then right. Old people getting down young people-style. Nasty.

"Y'all need to cut this mess out. I'm doing my homework!"

Mama froze for a second, and her eyes rolled up to mine in the mirror. At the start of the next bar, the rhythm hit her like lightning to a tree, and she said, "Hush up, boy. I heard your radio two minutes ago," then hunkered over, wagging her butt at me.

Laura yelled, "Aww naw!" and looked to see what I'd say, twisting her leg, doing the Tootsie Roll.

I couldn't think of nothing but, "Oh!"

Laura danced over, shooting her pointy elbows back so her breasts popped at me to the beat, and shut the door, blocking Mama's booty (Eww, Mama's booty) then her own laughing face. The funk sounded less fuzzy through the closed door. I went and cut on my Redman tape loud enough to drown their mess out. How could I erase my mind and get rid of what I'd just seen?

After one Redman verse, there was a knock on my door. Mama, warm and frizzy from dancing. My mouth was a storm of cuss words waiting to come crashing.

"Sorry 'bout that, baby."

Seeing Mama booty dance made me feel about a thousand years older, and the least horny that I'd been since sixth grade.

"We'll turn it down. But you need to cut that tape off and finish your homework."

Mama's jewelry box clapped shut in her room.

"What are y'all doing in there?"

What do girls do when they hang out? I figured it'd be more chill than that. Like maybe they put on lots of makeup then didn't move so they wouldn't smudge it.

"Laura was going through my closet," Mama's mouth shut, and she looked at the wall.

"For your date?"

"Yes. For that."

Laura appeared in the hall, grinning in some orangey-brown *Soul Train* BS.

"So, why him? Why this guy from work?"

I'd hoped Redman would make me feel tough, but next to his music, I just sounded whiny. I stepped back to hit Stop, and Mama followed me into the room. Laura looked from me to Mama and back, smiling, waiting for us to notice her get-up.

"He's nice. I like working with him, so I figure he might be fun to go out with. It's not like we're going to the wedding chapel."

I sat on the bed. Laura stepped into the doorway and thrust a hip forward, bouncing a pillow-sized turquoise purse. I was surprised I sounded a little hopeful when I asked, "You gonna get married again, Mama?"

Laura dropped her pose and stared with a hand on the purse clasp. I scooted toward my dresser as Mama sat at my desk, biggest schoolgirl ever.

"I don't know. I wouldn't mind it at some point, but it's way too soon to know, baby. 'sides, I got a lot on my hands."

She put both palms up, showing her invisible load, and asked, "Would you guys…want that?"

"Not if you left us here."

Why did I say that?

"Boy, she would take us too. We still kids!" Laura said, and looked at Mama to be sure she was right.

"I just don't wanna get left!"

Crying in my voice. Dang.

"For real, though," Laura said. "What are y'all gonna do Friday night?"

Mama sat straight in my chair all proud. "We're goin' to a concert."

Me and Laura nodded. I ain't gonna lie. I wanted to go to a concert.

5

These are the things I know about this Earnest MF that Mama's going on a date with:

Don't call a guy your Mama's going on a date with a MF. Think about it. Nasty.

They work together. He's a janitor.

He's a little, Jiminy Cricket-looking nigga with them creepy glasses that get raspberry jam-colored when he steps out into the sun.

His mop handle is taller than him.

He wears crackerish plaid shirts with a pack of cigarettes in the pocket that looks like a brick since the shirt and the rest of him are so small.

He says "Alright" all the time, instead of "Yes" and "Hello," and he draws it out long but doesn't say all the letters: "Awlll-ryyyyyyye."

"Alright, Kevin. How you doin' today?"

"Alright, nice weekend."

When it's time to go home, and he says a long "Alright," he bounces on his knees like he's a motor sneaking off farts.

Don't go spreading this around, but he's really funny. One time over Christmas, I was waiting by the car while Mama got something she forgot in the church daycare, and Earnest walked up next to me all casual and flipped off the back of the shack with the big nativity scene facing Cary St.

I was like, "What?" when I saw his bony finger in the air. He turned and shook his shoulders laughing, sharing the joke. And it was funny, knowing that on the other side of the shack's wall was some of those people from the congregation that call each other "Brother this" and "Sister that" like they all family, dressed up in shiny bathrobes, goo-gooing over a musty, black Cabbage Patch Kids doll, and they didn't know that ol' Earnest was giving them the bird.

He leaned against the driver's side door and popped a toothpick in his mouth. The shadow of his eyes gazed out over the church roof. Some fool drove by and honked at the nativity scene. Earnest said, "You know Damian?"

"No."

"I guess he a bitch."

The toothpick switched sides in his mouth. I couldn't help but smile at the cussing. Earnest said, "Someone wrote 'Damian a bitch' in that shack last night. Spent a hour scrubbing it out first thing this morning."

He looked at his scrubbing hands. Once I figured out he didn't think I'd done it, I laughed through my nose, like grown-ups. A little bit of laugh at someone writing that, and a little bit of laugh at how messed up it was that Earnest had to clean it.

"Damian a bitch," he repeated, like he'd never heard the b-word before. "Wish they'd get rid of that shack. Smell like pee in there."

Just as I was appreciating getting talked to like I was grown, Mama came back out the door, and Earnest stood straight, sliding up the car door.

"Don't go giving him no ideas," she joked to Earnest.

"Oh no, I was just cleaning your car." Earnest bent his knees doing the fart thing and rubbing his butt on the door. "Awlll-ryyyyyyye."

6

I don't know so much about Pop. It's more bits and pieces, filled in with a couple photos and what Laura remembers since she was around him two years longer. Here goes:

Superman angel Pop in white underpants and a v-neck, lying in a triangle patch of sun on the bedroom floor, doing sit-ups with his fingers laced into the back of his 'fro like stitches on a football.

Me with a dookie up my diaper to the small of my back, shaking the side of my crib like prison bars while he walks past the door going, "Slow your roll." Mama walks in a second later, comforting, to pick me up at arm's length.

He'd call Laura "Ms. La-La," and they had a baby-talk joke about how apartments don't have stairs.

I never lived in the apartment, but Laura says she remembers it, and sometimes Mama points it out when we drive by. You can see the fire escape from the avenue because they tore down the grocery that used to be across the alley. Whoever lives in the old apartment has kept a yellow-handled mop outside the back door for two years, and the kitchen window is so small that smells have to squeeze through. It's hard to picture big things happening in that apartment, like Mama and Pop still being in love, or baby Laura coming home from the hospital wrapped in a pink blanket like in the Polaroid.

They moved into our house when Mama was pregnant with me. She jokes that she carried me across the doorstep like newlyweds, but that's nasty.

The house has a concrete porch with a brick front. When you walk in through the front door, the living room's on your right. There's a fireplace with a mirror on the mantel and the green, flowered couch they brought from the apartment. I like to sit on it and pretend I'm Pop, with my whole life ahead of me.

Left of the fireplace is the dining room, where we eat dinner. The fourth chair is stacked with books and papers because it's where Mama does her nursing school homework. That could be Pop's seat, but my Pop is a pile of notebooks.

Straight back from the front door and phone table, through a low door, is the kitchen, with a dark green fridge, two-seat table, and daisy curtains that Mama's auntie bought before she died and left the house to Mama.

The kitchen's got the doors to the basement and backyard.

If you want to go upstairs, take a left from the front door. The hallway upstairs is kind of a circle, so when all the doors are closed, it looks like a Choose Your Own Adventure story up there.

The bathroom is over the kitchen, and Laura's bedroom faces the backyard, while Mama's bedroom faces front and is the biggest one with two windows. My bedroom is the smallest because I'm the youngest, even though I'm bigger than Laura. It's over the front door. Finally, the closet where Mama keeps the clipper set and extra bedsheets and towels kinda pokes out over the stairs.

When I can't hear the TV because Laura is stomping around the hall, mad at Mama, I sit on Pop's old couch and stare at the ceiling, wondering if she'll stomp through the floor, and burst through the ceiling with plaster dust and cracked boards. She'll bounce to the floor, then everything from her bedroom will tumble through the hole—lamps, boombox, shoes shoes shoes. The dresser will land on her face and kill her, and the blood will get wiped up by all the shirts that floated down like parachutes. You never know, it's a old house, from like World War II.

When Mama's driving me past a crowded sidewalk, I look for Pop. Same at the supermarket. I turn around to see if he's at the other end of the aisle, ten years older than the last picture with the orange shirt and narrow shoulders, holding a carton of oatmeal and staring at me. When I ask Mama where Pop is, she gets quiet then goes, "I don't know." She does the same when I ask if she ever talks to him.

This is what I'd ask Pop if I got to talk to him:

Do you still live in Richmond?

Do you have a house or a apartment?

Do you ever see us but don't say nothing?

I guess you ain't married because you would have told us, right?

Do you remember my birthday? Here's a hint: January 29, 1981.

Do you ever go to Fuddruckers?

Did you used to drive on DMV Drive when you were in high school?

What do you think about your old high school being closed down now and just being a bunch of spraypaint and crackheads?

Did you wish that would happen?

Why do people wanna smoke crack?

What kind of car do you have?

Here's what I'd tell Pop:

Even if you got married again, you're still me and Laura's pop.

I bet you could come over on my birthday. January 29.

I turned thirteen a couple months back. Mama took us to eat at Fuddruckers. You can put all you want on your burger. I like ketchup and mayonnaise because it tastes like pizza.

Laura's good. She's fifteen, and she said when she gets her license, we'll cruise slow on DMV drive.

Mama is good too. She's still real pretty, and she still works at the daycare at the church. Maybe you could bring her some lunch one day, from Lee's Famous, and you could talk about stuff, because she doesn't say a lot about you. Then, she could have some things to tell me.

Me and my friend David, who moved in up the street in first grade, are gonna be famous comedians like on *In Living Color*. We're gonna know a million jokes and make movies out of the skits from our TV shows. We practice telling jokes now, and we're really good. You've gotta see it.

You could have named me Tarvon, Jr.

Laura says she wants a Landcruiser.

OK, I admit, last year I wrote a bunch of that stuff in a letter to Pop and just put his name on the envelope, no address, and hoped it'd get to him. Maybe he was the mailman and would find it that way.

CHAPTER 6: THURSDAY

1

Kevin

The smell of paint and sweat hit my nose when I opened my gym locker. Doors were banging all around me, and Demetric's voice floated over from the next row, echoing off the concrete floor and high ceiling.

"Stinky finger, man."

Demetric's friend Maurice said, "Word?"

A bookbag *voop*ed open. Demetric said, "Yeah boy."

"With who?"

Maurice's voice got high-pitched and "who" hit a note on the ceiling. Something boomed into a locker. Demetric said, "Ain't tellin'."

"Nigga, you lyin'."

"Smell it."

Squeak of sneakers, persnickety voice, Maurice: "Get your finger out my face."

I stood there, staring into my dark locker. Heard the little jingle of a belt unbuckling. Demetric said, "Hey man, proof's on the finger."

Lucky MF. Demetric is in the smart classes, but people don't clown him because he's cool. Let me try that sometime.

Maurice is Demetric's old friend who didn't get as popular in middle school. He said, "You just want me to take your lyin'-ass word for it."

Loud sniffing sound. Maurice said, "Chimp-ass nigga standing there smelling his own finger."

I didn't want to rustle my clothes and drown out their conversation, but standing there in my boxers was getting weird.

Demetric said, "Mmm! Someone's gotta smell it."

He sounded casual, like he went around fingering girls every week. I hate thinking this, but it's true: I haven't even kissed anyone yet, and here goes Demetric getting to third. When's my time gonna come?

"Ha-ha," Maurice was laughing. "I ain't slappin' your hand. Who knows if you washed it since!"

"I used my other hand anyway."

There was the clap of them giving each other five. I stepped into my gym shorts. My sweaty socks were cool on the floor.

"Who was it? For real."

"Aint' telling right now. But we got at it on the couch," Demetric snickered.

Maurice hooted. Who was it? Demetric probably knew some girls at other schools. Didn't see any girl walking around our school looking like they just got fingered.

More guys came into the locker room, and I sped up, not wanting to hang out half-dressed. As I was digging around in my bag looking for my gym shirt, it hit me—the shirt was still on my bedroom floor, where I'd ditched it after Mama caught me lip-synching to Eddie Murphy. If you don't dress out once, you get a warning. Twice, you get a detention. Same with the third time. You get in-school on the fourth, and on your fifth time, you fail. This was my first miss. Maybe I'd only get half a warning since I had my shorts. Mr. Bisceglia might not even notice. He was known to miss all sorts of cheating because he stayed busy looking at the bottom of Chiffawn Marion's booty poking out her rolled-up shorts.

I walked out slow to the gym, not looking forward to PE class. Hip-hop was playing on Mr. B's boombox, loud enough to just be static and drums slapping the cinderblock walls. Mr. B hates rap. Once he called it "Crap with a silent 'C'," and it took us a minute to get the joke, then still, no one laughed. He usually puts on a rock 'n' roll station with songs that he liked back when he had all his hair. Every now and then, we have to hit a volleyball around while he plays some country BS with some cracker singing about the Ku Klux Klan or whatever.

The gym was alive without Mr. B, and it was exciting in the same way that knowing you're about to tell someone off is—kinda dangerous. I love the music and that no rules/no teachers feeling, but I'm definitely not good enough at ball to jump into the pickup game before the bell. Tyrell, Leo, and two other guys were playing half court, balling rough and close between the free-throw line and the basket, hardly passing, just shooting, shoving each other for the rebound, then shooting again. The paint was so crowded with big dudes that each shot looked like the ball had squeezed out between their bodies and popped into the air. They weren't sinking many baskets.

I heard, "'sup, Mushy Tushy?" as Demetric trotted past me and joined the game. I don't mind when he jokes because he keeps it between us, instead of trying to put me on blast. I watched his fingers spread as he dribbled the ball. Had he washed them since yesterday? Did they still smell? Was he getting the smell on the ball? Whose smell was it? Do they smell different from each other?

Mr. Bisceglia followed his belly into the gym,

wearing black sweatpants and a Dallas Cowboys t-shirt and carrying a maroon can of Tab soda. I picked at the bottom of my blue t-shirt and hoped Mr. B wouldn't notice it. The neon lights in the cages high up on the ceiling reflected off Mr. B's bald spot as he bent to click off the tape, then blew his whistle for everyone's attention. Leo took one last shot, off the backboard and through the hoop, and Mr. B blew the whistle again, harder. The players all turned, and the ball left the net swinging, then bounced into the corner.

Mr. B clapped his hands and said, "Alright everybody, basketball today. Let's get four teams going."

Basketball is all the guys' favorite sport. Guess it's mine, too, but I'm no good at it.

Reading down the attendance sheet, Mr. B separated teams by pointing people to different corners of the gym. The two groups on the right hit the bleachers, and my team and the other took opposite ends of the court while Mr. B fiddled with the boombox until some rock 'n' roll that sounded like a beer commercial came on. Tyrell took center for the other team. I stood near Demetric, looking away, but sniffing in his direction. I didn't smell nothing but that gym smell of old sweat and floor varnish.

Mr. B blew the whistle, his favorite thing in the world. Demetric trotted to the center for the tipoff, and tapped my shoulder, "You on defense."

I smelled my shirt. *Which hand did he use?* Nothing. I walked to the side of the free-throw line and stood with my knees bent, hands on thighs, looking ready, but already sending my mind out to think about important things, hoping the ball wouldn't come my way.

Don't take this wrong, but in gym class, sometimes I wish I'm a girl. That way, no one would expect me to do nothing but get flustered when the ball comes at me. I could scrunch my face and throw it badly and things would work out fine. That's about what I usually do anyway, but, if I was a girl, no one would care. No one would hit my arm and go, "You messed up," and hey, I could go into the girls' locker room after class and watch them change.

The guys took all the forward positions and played a lot of defense, too. They moved up and down the court in a cluster while me and the other three people stood back and acted like we were ready to jump in so Mr. B wouldn't blow the whistle at us. I was just passing my time until the game ended, hoping my team would lose so we wouldn't have to play whoever won the next game.

Mr. Bisceglia calls this, "Elimination, bracket-style," and shouts things from the sideline like, "C'mon, Final Four!" That man is corny.

Things were going OK. The ball hadn't come my

way, and Mr. B hadn't said nothing about my blue shirt. My team was shooting on the basket, and I was at center court, pretending it was the middle of the world, when Tyrell broke out to catch a wide rebound and came dribbling upcourt, right at me.

The rock music and the squeak of gym shoes and Chiffawn's honey-coated legs dropped away, leaving me, Tyrell the charging bull, and that dark orange ball booming off the floor as it got closer. Sweat dripped off the tip of Tyrell's nose and sprayed to the sides with each breath. I remembered throwing the lit cigar all the way onto Tyrell's balcony and stopped being shook. Tyrell could be got. And I could get him, starting with this basketball. I crouched down, really ready.

Tyrell was set to pass five feet to my right with his eyes locked on the hoop. I'll be real, I'm bad at sports, but Tyrell acting like I wasn't even there did not fly with me. I spread my arms into a defense position and cut back diagonally. By the three-point line, I leaned in right as Tyrell popped his arms up for a jumper, and elbowed the side of my head. My face mashed on the sweaty front of his gym shirt.

Most guys bring their PE clothes home every week or two to put them in the laundry, but not Tyrell. And that shirt stank, like cabbagey old sweat, tobacco smoke, and oily body smells. Tyrell made a deep woofing noise and landed a couple feet to the left, grabbing his knees for balance. I spun away, eyes stinging from Tyrell's sweat, and had to run three steps to keep from falling. I stopped in the paint and, over the ringing in my head, heard someone on the bleachers yell, "Dag!"

I clapped a hand to my ear, which felt all hot. The ball landed in front of the hoop, bounced off the wall, and rolled to a stop by Tyrell's woolly mammoth feet. He picked it up and whipped it off my side. The air in the ball rang when it hit. I doubled over. The heat flashed in my shoulders and forehead, then turned icy at my toes. I'd been elbowed in the head, hit in the ribs with a ball, had the wind knocked out of me, and never fingered anyone. Plus, Tyrell was hopping on his toes next to me, yelling, "Mr. B! He fouled me, Mr. B! I need a free throw!"

The people on the bleachers started shuffling around, murmuring, and I felt all of their eyes on me. The basketball was stopped on the floor, halfway between me and Tyrell, sitting there stupid like it had no idea of the grief it was causing. Tyrell was still carrying on about free throws. I looked at how his belly bounced while he hopped on his toes and hated him more than I hated anyone since third grade, when I realized Pop wasn't coming back. No Tyrell would equal no problems. I yelled, "You fouled *me*, man!"

And, like always happens when I get mad, my

voice moved from a croak to a squeak, and I clapped my lips shut. I'd never yelled in class. Tyrell got blurry, and I automatically reached both hands up to wipe my eyes, then realized that I looked like a crying cartoon baby with tears shooting out. Everyone was watching, necks cocked, eyes wide, mouths hanging. For a second, I felt proud of showing the room that I could be bad too, but then I realized they thought I was crying. I wasn't. It was silent in the room, but there'd be noise any second.

Mr. B must have been shocked because he just looked back and forth between me and Tyrell, who had his palms up like "What?" and said, "You guys both fouled each other. Let's do a tip off with … Demetric and Leo." He gave his head a tiny shake, then clapped twice and boomed, "Come on everybody, heads in the game!"

As Tyrell turned to go to the tipoff, he called me a bitch. I was moving back near the free-throw line when Mr. B went, "Wait, Kevin. That's not your gym shirt."

I felt lit up by the whole class's eyes. I took a big breath that shook when I exhaled.

"I know."

Mr. B tucked the basketball against his hip like a mama carrying a baby and said, "Why didn't you dress out?"

"I did."

I pointed at the Richmond Public Schools logo on my red shorts.

"But where's your shirt? You've gotta dress out all the way to play."

Mr. B stood center court, like he ran the whole world. A guitar solo started on the boombox. His hand moved to the whistle around his neck. I said, "Well, I'm already playing."

He couldn't write me up halfway through class for being halfway dressed. It wasn't like I'd not dressed out so I wouldn't have to play. I'd really tried. Demetric looked at the clock behind the cage on the wall and hissed his teeth. Tyrell rocked his head side to side, stretching his neck, a pleased look on his sweaty face.

"Not anymore. Sit down!"

Mr. B stomped his right foot and pointed to the bleachers. The whistle swung back and forth. I hated him so bad right then. He hadn't been good enough at sports to go pro, and he'd never even be good enough at watching them to be a ref, so this was all he got. He just got to boss around middle school kids who he thought were too young to tell how much of a loser he was.

"Fine by me. I ain't wanna play gay-ass basketball anyway."

I heard my voice echo and made a beeline for the bleachers, which got blurry.

"What did you say?" Mr. Bisceglia thundered.

I kept walking. Mr. B blasted his whistle. Chiffawn laughed, "He said basketball gay, Mr. B."

Thanks, Chiffawn.

Tyrell got back in the mix and yelled, "Basketball ain't gay!"

Crap. If I said basketball was gay, that meant the people who played it were gay, too. And what did Tyrell, and all of the other really big dudes, like to do? Play basketball. So, I'd just called Tyrell, Leo, and every other big dude at school gay.

"Aww!"

A rustle and a holler went up through the class, with kids yelling and stomping on the bleachers. Mr. B dropped the ball and came trotting after me, so I headed for the cool, quiet locker room.

I heard the basketball being dribbled and shot off the backboard. Footsteps squeaked behind me.

"Basketball ain't gay. *You* gay!" Tyrell yelled.

Mr. B stopped and pointed at Tyrell, "You. Office. Now."

I started for the locker room door again, then stopped when I felt Mr. B's hand on my shoulder. Tyrell was ranting and raving like Taz on the cartoons as he walked across the gym and shoved open the door to the hall. Mr. B said, "Kevin. What the hell?"

His cracker accent made "hell" into two syllables, "hay-ull." He circled around front of me and leaned in, speaking quietly in a buddy-buddy tone, like I'd let him down somehow. Chiffawn's hair, forehead, then eyes peeked over the side of the bleachers.

I looked at the locker room door three feet beyond Mr. B. and wanted to push past him. He said, "You're never like this. What's goin' on?"

His breath was hot and sour. The skin on his forehead was rougher than the smooth part where his hair used to be.

"Nothing. I just ... left my shirt at home."

"You can't talk like that in class ('clay-uss'). Or anywhere."

He leaned back a little and swept out his right arm, pointing out the entire world that would be mad if I called basketball "gay" again. I wanted the world to be bigger than just the gym.

"OK. I dressed out as much as I could."

I couldn't say sorry to this man, because I didn't mean it. This man, with his diet soda and his eyes that look at the girls who are twenty years younger than him. This man, who runs the class that I hate the most.

"I see. But I've still gotta write you up, Kevin. You can't act like that in class."

He looked sorry to be writing me up. But if he was really sorry, he wouldn't do it. I hated his bushy eyebrows that were almost as big as his stupid black mustache and how he was pretending to feel sorry.

And getting written up? Man. That meant he'd call home and talk to Mama, and I'd get grounded for even longer and wouldn't be able to go see *The Mask* on Saturday. I hung my head, away from Mr. B's face and breath. He took his hands off my shoulders and clapped my back.

"Hit the locker room and get changed, Kevin. Stay on the bleachers for the rest of the class."

The locker room was gray and quiet. I passed Demetric's row. Had his stinky finger touched a locker handle? I wanted to smell and see if I could tell which one was his, and if it really smelled like fish.

Getting written up was for bad kids. I'm not a bad kid. I don't go around getting in trouble, but it seemed like trouble had been getting into me.

Everything I did echoed alone. I took my time changing, sitting in my boxers on the wood bench, trying to figure out what to do about the phone call coming after school. Nevermind Tyrell.

2

We had to finish our science lab from Tuesday. Aisha sat next to me, and I could feel her there even though we weren't touching. I thought a thousand tiny messages that I wanted to sink through her skin. *Kevin is fly. His tushy is not mushy. You want to go out with him. He'd be the illest boyfriend.* I was high on my stool, butt pulled in to hide any mushiness.

Mr. Gordon was talking slow, like we're dumb. He held up a knobby finger and said, "Roll the ball from the first mark on the wedge. Then," he held up another finger, "roll the ball from the second mark on the wedge."

We're not dumb. We've just got better things to do than science.

Demetric peeked across the aisle and whispered, "Wedge," drawing out the middle, "Wayyyydge," and it hit me funny. I held in the laugh until I started bouncing on my stool, eyes watering, finally cooling down after PE.

I stood at the end of the table with my knees bent and my butt pointed away from Aisha, catching the ball as it rolled off the wedge. Aisha's jacket smelled like English muffins, which got me tripping on how I like to pull them apart instead of cutting them, so they're scratchier when they come out the toaster. The ball rolled under the radiator, and I felt my booty poking out when I went to get it. Aisha tapped my back with a ruler, six inches from my mushy tushy, and said, "Here, use this."

"Thanks."

When I stood up with the ball, Aisha was watching Demetric coming from the corner of the room, curling a long, cardboard tube like a dude lifting weights. He said, "We could blast the balls with this."

As soon as he said, "balls," our eyes met, and we got to laughing again. Aisha shook her head, but I could tell she thought we were funny. Demetric was cackling while he put the tube in front of his pants and started humping the air, going, "YIT-YEAH! You know it's true."

I wished he'd hit the tube on the edge of the table and spear himself in the nuts.

He turned his hips and pointed the tube across my lap, at Aisha's face. I got kinda horny and mad. Demetric said, "You don't know 'bout my dick, Kevin."

"Course I don't know about your—"

Aisha pushed the tube back out over the table, then said, "He don't have to know to guess. 'sides, we all know, it's the quiet ones you gotta look out for."

Then she turned to me, put three fingers on my hoodie sleeve and said, "Ain't that right, Kevin?"

Even if I did get wild in PE today, I'm a quiet one. I blinked, cheesed, and looked up the tube, from Aisha to Demetric. Right then, I figured that keeping to myself ain't bad after all. And that loud dudes make a lot of noise, but noise ain't nothing but something to irritate people. And that what Aisha had just said balanced out that mushy tushy BS. And that I'd be calling her after school, trying to sound casual. And, finally, I decided that Mama would never wash this hoodie again.

I looked at the dent from her fingers on my sleeve, almost heart-shaped, then nodded, slow as she shook her head before.

3

David wanted me to come try out Mario Paint, but I told him Mama was around, so I couldn't sneak out. Really, I needed to deal with the message from school and call Aisha.

Tyrell called me a faggot for sitting next to David on the bus. I thought about how, in about an hour, I'd be going out with Aisha and would have cold, hard proof that I'm not gay.

At home, I wondered if I should leave the front door open so Ms. Ransom across the street could see me jumping in the air when Aisha said, "Yes." She's gonna say, "Yes."

The green light was blinking on the answering machine. I listened to the house for a second to make sure no one was home, then hit play. It was the school secretary, an old, white lady.

"Hello Ms. Phifer, this is Sondra Threadgill calling from the office at Henderson Middle School. Kevin got written up today in PE class, and we need you to call the office before he is allowed to go back to PE. The number here is (804)..."

I hit the delete button and backed away, making

sure I hadn't moved anything around. How long is Aisha's bus ride home? Didn't wanna be stuck pacing the house, waiting to get a girlfriend.

I could see her yellow cheese bus rumbling up some narrow, Northside street. She sat alone, looking peaceful in a green vinyl seat. She had no idea she was about to have her world rocked.

I went to the bathroom and stood at the mirror. Would having a girlfriend make me more of a man? Would my goatee fill in the middle of my chin? I flicked the bathroom light switch super-fast like the strobe at a school dance and bobbed my head, beatboxing. When me and Aisha start going out, we'll slow dance in the ocean-green lights when the DJ plays Boyz II Men. I shimmied until I got winded and the light made me dizzy. Was Aisha home yet? Soon.

Should I make some food for energy? I broke up a cheese slice on some crackers and played the conversation I was about to have with Aisha in my head.

She'd say, "What up Kevin?"

"Kickin' it."

That worked. Cool guys kick it. But I had to ask her about her. I swallowed a cracker, sipped OJ from the carton and decided I'd say, "Whatchoo doin'?"

"I'm kickin' it too."

"Cool."

What was kickin' it for Aisha? Some TV shows?

Microwave popcorn? A dollhouse? A couple friends by?

Kickin' it for me ain't all that different, except for the dollhouse. And, a couple friends is just me and David, rewinding the Homer parts from that week's *Simpsons*. Somehow, when Aisha kicked it, it seemed a lot more fly. But that's what's good about her. She does the same things, but she does them good.

My tongue pulled the last bits of cheese from my teeth, and I walked back to the phone table hearing the scary, Darth Vader classical music from *Star Wars* in my head. My life would be different after I called a girl for the first time. After I asked a girl out. After she said, "Yes," and I wasn't stuck on the block watching cartoons with David, who got all worked if I put a foot on his mama's coffee table.

But what if she said, "No?" What if she told everyone at school? Then, the second I stepped on the bus, I'd get clowned right and left by all those eighth graders who had popped out of their mamas feeling girls up.

Can't dwell on that, though. I opened the phone book to page one forty-eight, even though I know her number. It seemed like the right thing to do, like in a movie. If she said, "No," I'd have to remember to close the book again so Mama wouldn't see it open and start asking squinty questions about who I was calling and how the great girlfriend search was going.

Lord. But there was no way Aisha would say, "No."

So, I'd stand at the table and call Aisha, and she'd say, "Yes," and I'd ask her to go to the movies that weekend, and we'd make plans, and I'd go upstairs and jerk off for the first of two hundred and thirty three times thinking about what it would be like sitting next to Aisha in a dark room. Would she smell like English muffins? The light from the projection booth will shine through her hair and gleam off her puffy cheeks. What will it be like when she leans into me after I put my arm around her? How far into the movie should I put my arm around her? Hot damn, I'm gonna put my arm around her.

My nerves were clanging, and I rattled the number into the phone so fast there was a two-hour pause before it started ringing.

One ring.

I'd give it six rings.

Two rings.

Most people's answering machines came on after four.

Three rings.

More than six rings was rude if she couldn't get to the phone because she was in the bathroom or something.

Four rings.

Didn't want her all mad when I got her on the phone.

There was a click.

What would I say on the message? Couldn't go asking girls out on their answering machines. Someone might play the tape on the loudspeaker at school. Forget all that.

A slow, old man voice said, "Hello."

I waited for him to say, "You've reached the Billups residence. Leave a message."

Instead, he said, "Hello?" again.

I said, "Aisha there?" real fast so he wouldn't hang up.

"'scuse me?"

I remembered my manners and spoke slow, like batteries dying.

"May I please speak to Aisha?"

"Aisha?"

"Aisha...Billups?"

What if this was the wrong number? A girl as fine as Aisha might need to have an unlisted number.

"She ain't live here. This her granddaddy."

The old man was country as all get out. I was surprised he had a real phone instead of a soup can and some string. A delivery truck rumbled up my block.

"Ohh."

Dang. What now?

"What you want with her?"

"She's one of my friends from school. I...had a

question about some homework."

I'm a lousy liar and was glad that the old man couldn't see me bopping back and forth, pulling faces while I thought of what to say.

"Ohh. You ain't got that number from some school list? I don't study giving out my family's phone numbers to strangers."

"No. We don't got a list like that."

We hadn't had one since grade school. What did this old guy know?

"Alright then. Hold the phone please."

There was a knock as the old guy set the phone down, then I heard him shuffle off, open a drawer, and shuffle back. "You there, young man?"

"Yeah."

"'Yes'. You say 'Yes' when you talking to your elders."

"Yes." I threw in a "sir" for good measure. Old man probably saluted Union soldiers in the Civil War.

"OK. You got a purnsil?"

I grabbed the pen sitting on the table.

"Yes sir."

"It's three-too-nahn...oh-nahn, nahn-won."

"Thank you, sir."

I smiled into the phone. Maybe one day I'll meet him and thank him.

"You welcome, young man."

The numbers were blue train cars across the page.

I had to call her before her grandpa did and started fussing about, "Some boy called here looking for you. Had to learn him how to address his elders. You been giving this number out to all types of trash?"

Would she know it was me? Would she hope so?

I dialed the new number. The scene I'd made up, of Aisha on the couch by the phone, started to play out. But after four rings, there was a click, then a younger man's voice, echoing across an empty room, told me to leave a message.

"Hey Aisha, it's Kevin from school. Gimme a call."

4

After I hung up, I felt wrung out. I went upstairs, put Redman on quiet so I could hear the phone, and started thinking about the call from school. No PE until Tuesday, so I had some time. I could even go see *The Mask*, then tell Mama about the phone call on Monday. I need to get out of the house before I get grounded all over again. Need to see *The Mask*. Need to go on a date with Aisha. After tonight, maybe I could say, "Go on a date," like it was something I had to do. "This weekend, I've gotta rake the yard, go to some BS at Mama's job, and go on a date."

Redman's my favorite rapper because he's funny. He's not just a gangster or a lover-man, but I can tell he can knock some heads or land a lady when the time comes. I sat on my bed, bouncing to the beat until the mattress springs started squeaking, and wondered if me and Aisha would squeak some bedsprings. We'd have to kiss first. Things move in order, like how Demetric was saying his old girlfriend made him wait a month before he fingered her, and then she was gonna blow him a month later, but she broke up with him a week before. Whenever her name comes up, he goes, "She owes me one!"

Rap tapes always have a bunch of guys in the studio, talking between songs, doing a verse, or just getting a shout-out at the end of a track. It would be dope to make an album and get the crew, jokes and nicknames that come with it. My rap name would be King Kev, but all I got is David, some *Simpsons* quotes, and the nickname "Choo-Choo."

Corey gave me the Redman tape. Laura and him broke up around Thanksgiving after a whole week where The Funkmobile didn't pull up in front of the house, and Laura would always jiggle the answering machine cord to see if it was plugged in.

She went to a party the weekend before, and Mama let her stay out until twelve since it was nearby. I was in my room, just after eleven, when I heard the front door slam and Mama go, "What's wrong, baby?"

Saturday Night Live was about to come on. When I went downstairs, Laura was crying on Mama's shoulder on the couch. Before she left, she'd spent an hour hissing hairspray in the bathroom, and now she was smashing down her 'do on Mama.

I remember cold water in my socks from a puddle by Laura's shoes and wishing I could point the TV remote at Laura and Mama and fast forward until they went upstairs.

But something in the way Laura curled against Mama, with Mama sprinkling her fingers on Laura's shoulder, made me think it was a bad idea to bug them. So, I went back upstairs and piled Corey's tapes on my bed, wanting to listen to them all at once because I was scared I'd have to give them back.

Laura stayed in her room until dinner the next day. She wore yellow pajamas at the table, and Mama'd made Laura's favorite—mac 'n' cheese with ham pieces. I like that plenty, too, but this mac 'n' cheese tasted funny, like it didn't belong to me. Had three plates anyway.

After all that, I never saw Corey again, I had to tape songs off the radio, and Laura stopped talking to her best friend, Sharese, which was a shame because I'd just started realizing that Sharese was fine as all get out.

Our street's as wide as three cars. One parked on each side, with a little sliver for people to drive through. When someone with a boomin' system is cruising, the thumping bass starts blocks away, shaking car alarms to life. Everything gets louder and louder until the house windows rattle. The Redman song ended, and I heard someone out front. A silver car was stopped. The driver had a big, black t-shirt and skinny arms. The left one was on the wheel, holding a cigarette. Smoke splashed upside down inside the windshield. Legs in baggy jeans spread on the seat, and the car roof cut off his face. The girl in the passenger seat was Laura. I knew the black jacket and red jeans she'd just got after fussing at Mama. The driver's right hand lifted off his thigh and swung over toward Laura, who scooted in. Their bodies stayed close while something started to glow and tickle inside of me, then the driver's hand grabbed Laura's chest. She cupped her hand over his, then put it on the gear shifter. I guess they kept kissing, but I couldn't see, and that was probably for the better. It was weird to watch Laura get felt on when just the idea of breasts is enough for a hard-on, but my sister ain't the same at all. I just felt kinda nasty and couldn't look anymore, so I clicked off the tape and ran downstairs to the dining room table, half a hard-on bouncing against my leg with each step.

5

When Laura came in, I looked up, blinking and smiling like I'd been deep into studying. I wasn't sure what to say, but I knew I needed her help.

"What are you smiling at, Kevin?"

"My favorite sister!"

"Mmm-hmm."

Her forehead frowned, but the rest of her face was smiling.

"Laura, uhh, I need your help."

I pushed my chair back to stand, remembered my chubby, and leaned forward with my elbows on the table.

"Like I don't have enough homework of my own."

She shook her bookbag.

"No, um…"

I needed to catch her while she was still happy. I decided to be straight-up. A straight line is quickest, like in Physics.

"I'm not allowed to go back to PE until Mama calls the office."

I sounded like a baby for having these problems.

"Boy, what did you do?"

"I didn't dress out, then I fussed at the teacher."

It sounded stupid now. Laura rolled her eyes and laughed like she was so much better than middle school, less than a year later. I didn't say nothing, though.

"Mr. B?"

"Yeah."

She wrinkled her nose, remembering him, then

said, "So, what you want me to do?"

I pointed at the phone. "I want you to...sound like Mama."

"You crazy," she said, waving a hand and turning for the stairs. I stood up. The chubby was gone, and I kinda had to piss.

"Come on. I can't be stuck around here grounded all weekend, too!"

She stopped. Her shoulders sank as she breathed out.

"Alright. But you're gonna owe me big. You're right, though. I can't have you getting on my nerves all weekend."

I followed her over to the phone.

"What's the number?"

"Dang. I erased it off the answering machine."

"Did anyone else call after that?"

"No."

"Then it's still on the tape. Hold up."

Laura was like a TV detective, leaning over the answering machine, poking buttons and sliding up the volume. I pretended we were checking out evidence, about to catch a murderer. She reached for the pen and paper.

"No! Hold up."

She popped up her head at me. Ms. Threadgill's voice came on. I ran into the dining room and grabbed my notebook.

"Let me write it here so Mama don't see it on the pad."

We got the number, and I stood in the kitchen door, scheming on sneaking over to David's to call our machine and record over Ms. Threadgill's message.

Cool as anything, Laura called the school, standing with her hip leaned to the left and the phone cradled on her left shoulder. It was like Saturday Night Laura had mixed with my sister and turned into exactly what I needed. It better work.

"Hello. Ms. Threadgill, please."

Laura pronounced every letter, using the same voice that Mama uses when she calls someone important, like the electric company or the deacon at her work.

"Hiii, yes, this is Sheila Phifer, Kevin Phifer's mother."

I had to look up and make sure Mama hadn't just appeared. Laura paused, grabbed the phone with her right hand, and turned toward me, avoiding my eyes. She even had Mama's look on her face, nodding while this slow, southern accent came tinny out the earpiece. I stepped in to listen.

"Ms. Phifer," Ms. Threadgill said, "your son got written up in PE today. In the report, Mr. Bisceglia said…"

I wondered if Aisha was trying to call back and getting a busy signal.

"Kevin didn't dress out, and called basketball... 'gay.'"

Laura stood straight and bobbled the phone between her hands, finally clamping it against her ribs as she turned away and snorted out a laugh. A "Hello?" came creaking from the phone.

"Yes. I'm sorry... my allergies are acting up."

Ms. Threadgill was silent, and I stared at the phone, willing her to not catch on. Laura pressed on.

"So, can Kevin go back to Mr. B—Bisceglia's class?"

"Ma'am, we just require the phone call, in the hopes that you will talk to your son."

"Oh, I will," said Laura, deep and ominous. "He'll definitely be on punishment." Laura pointed at the staircase and let her hand drift off, resting it on her right side. I got happy and had to check myself—was I glad to be going back to PE?

Laura hung up and turned to me, herself again. "Boy, you said basketball gay?"

I started to think of an explanation, then Laura bent with one hand on the phone and the other balled up in front of her laughing mouth. It got me going, too. I slapped the table and dropped my head, shaking with laughter.

Paul

Paul was sitting on the gray stairs, resting his dogs, when he heard the door push open a flight down, then four sneakers shuffling, the rustle of clothes, a girl's giggle, and the smacking of lips on lips. Paul sighed and rolled his eyes to the ocean-green four on the wall. His thighs ached as he stood. He hated the staircase. Without it, the job would be OK. Pass the day by walking around the museum, keeping children from getting too hands-on with the weather exhibits, and pacing the grounds outside, eye peeled for graffiti and cars that shouldn't be parked.

Then, the stairs happened. With one cigarette drag on the third floor landing, a high school kid set off the fire alarm. Fire trucks careened into the turnaround and sped up to the museum door. The whole building evacuated onto the museum lawn, where the rush of escape was stopped by a gray, February morning. Adults squinted at Broad St. and shifted, foot-to-foot, in the grass. Clusters of kids broke off to play tag, freezing when the men in rubber suits emerged, having found the Doral stubbed out on the stairs, bent like a crashed plane.

Paul had never thought of himself as an authority figure, but after the first group of teenagers stiffened upon his approach, he learned that if you're tall, black, silent, and in uniform—Steady Paul on the job—people don't tend to play with you. Except cops, who think security guards are wannabes.

A smug, white officer stood at Paul's left hand, and a firefighter pinched the offending cigarette at his right.

"You didn't see this happening?" the cop asked, holding back a laugh.

Making it worse, the police were salty because the museum didn't employ off-duty cops. They used to, but too many second-jobbers were divorcees with child support to pay who napped in the little theaters. Paul pursed his lips and looked from the cigarette, to the cop's red cheeks, to the fan of kids craning to see what was going on.

"I was about to go on break when this call came in," the cop said, wistful.

"Well, they started selling Krispy Kreme at the 7-11 up Boulevard," Paul said, throwing a thumb over his shoulder. "Maybe you can get up there before your break run out."

The cop glared at Paul, trying to think of a way to get the last word. Finally, he said, "You just do your job, security guard. Maybe next time the fire trucks won't come so fast," then put a hand on his walky-talky, swiveled on a heel, and strutted to his car, a jiggling Batman. The firefighter turned to his truck.

A wave of people filtered through the tall, museum

doors. Paul's boss, Walton, summoned him with a walky-talky crackle.

"Phifer, we're adding the stairwell to your route. We need you to walk those stairs at least twice a shift, three times when we've got student groups. We can't have that happening again."

Paul loomed over Walton, trying to imagine his lazy ass walking the stairs. He'd probably slip in his own sweat and break his neck. Then Paul could quit and…do what? The problem with a bad job is that your next job will probably be bad too. They all are, in their own ways.

The stairs made Paul's thighs grape jelly, and he took to zoning out and resting when he was supposed to be walking. This time, he was imagining himself and Xavier at a resort where the umbrellas in their cocktails matched their blue-striped beach umbrella, when he heard the kids making out. Paul leaned against the railing and looked through the little corner in-between his flight and the next one down. Baggy jeans and black Nikes faced the wall while tight jeans and orange Etonics backed against it. Two mouths slurped. Paul took deliberate steps across the landing, slapping his shoes to announce his approach. Below him, the smacking stopped, and the girl whispered, "Hey."

"Hmm?" grumbled a deeper voice.

Paul stepped again, savoring the echo.

"Hear that?" the girl asked.

"Whuh?"

Paul was halfway down the next flight of stairs. He stopped, cleared his throat, and jangled the massive tangle of keys on his belt.

"That."

The boy sucked his teeth and said, "Damn."

The girl sounded urgent and frightened.

"Let's go."

Paul stepped onto the landing above them as the girl disappeared through the door. The boy hunched and scowled, trying to look mean while hiding the swelling in his baggy jeans. He grunted, "'choo lookin' at, pervert?" before catching the swinging door and popping back into the museum. Paul rolled his eyes, glad he didn't have to say anything, and walked another flight to the ground floor. This was work, like telling people they needed to drop a couple hundred on a new muffler was his pop's work, like dealing with barking dogs on the mail route was his grandpa's work. What else could work be?

In the cafeteria, Angela stuck out her chest and winked as she slid his free hot chocolate across the counter. Extra marshmallows jiggled back and forth at the top of the cup.

7
Kevin

I was at my desk with me and Mama's doors open so I could run for the phone. Aisha was gonna call any minute, and I didn't want Laura to get it first and say something corny like, "It's for you Kevin...it's a girl."

In the kitchen, silverware was clanking, and Uncle Paul and Laura were joking. Then, Paul went, "OK," and his heavy footsteps started up the stairs. Mama walks heavy because she's tired. Uncle Paul does because he's a man, and people need to know he's coming. I'd only stared at my homework, but it wouldn't matter soon, when Paul was proud of me for getting out there with the ladies. Wish we'd been talking about girls instead of Mama in Chimborazo Park.

Paul hopped into my room and started rubbing on the back of my head until it burned, joking, "Big K! How's the cut?"

Paul picks his short 'fro whenever he takes off his hat. I patted down the little bit of hair on the back of my head and said, "Cool, cool. It's good."

"I knew Xavier would get you right."

Hmm. Xavier.

"Yeah. You go to that barber a lot?" I asked.

"Every now and then. He's not my usual barber, but he's a friend of mine."

"Oh."

Paul leaned on the doorframe. Why is he friends with a gay guy? What do they do together? How does Paul handle getting hit on by him?

"What's it like being friends with … him?"

Paul froze, like a cat about to bolt.

"It's cool, Big K. It's cool."

Light from the window made little flashes on his glasses. I couldn't see his eyes, but I was pretty sure he wasn't looking at me.

"But that barber, he gay, right?"

Uncle Paul turned his head, and I could see his eyes pointed at the lamp on my desk.

"Yeah, far as I know he is."

I had my ideas about this boy from grade school named Teddy, who always stuck out a hip when he was standing, and that shorthaired lady at the grocery store, but I'd never been sure that I'd met a gay person. As far as Paul knew? How far did Paul know?

"If you think he gay, why'd you take me to him?"

Uncle Paul sighed, shifted his feet, and dragged his thumb and forefinger across his brow to pinch above his nose.

"Kevin. Was everyone in that barber shop gay?"

I clapped my hands over my head. Paul held up a hand.

"OK. No, they weren't. But all those people were there because Xavier is a good barber. He did a terrific job with your cut."

I started to smile. Paul said, "It shouldn't matter if he's gay or not."

"But what if someone saw me in his chair and thinks I'm a faggot?"

Two seconds of quiet. That word had slipped out because talking to Uncle Paul is like talking to a friend, not a grown-up. That's the weird, cool thing about Uncle Paul.

"Who would say that, Kevin?"

"I dunno. Girls. Someone at school."

"Kevin, don't worry about it, man."

I wasn't worrying about nothing. This was the truth. Aisha better call back and say, "Yes."

Paul said, "I mean, just, keep doing your thing. There's always gonna be someone wanna say something, so just do you."

But I've been doing me and it ain't working. And if people started saying things, wasn't no way Aisha would say, "Yes."

"Look, K. The haircut doesn't make you look gay. But there's nothing wrong with being gay. Don't worry."

What!

"You think I'm gay?" I asked.

"I ... Kevin ... Look, man. I'm grown, right? I'm your uncle, and I've known you since you were born. And sometimes, you're not gonna wanna hear this, but…"

I dare him to insult me. Paul spread his hands in front of him like he was keeping a dog back.

"…sometimes I forget how old you are. Seems like just yesterday that you were walking for the first time."

Man wasn't answering my question.

"So, you think I'm gay?"

"No," he finally answered. Paul's hands dropped to his sides. "I hadn't even thought of you dating yet."

Why not? One of the reasons Paul is the man is because he acts like I'm the man, too. Had he been faking? Am I so wack that no one believes I'll go out with girls? Just wait until Aisha calls back.

"When did you start dating?"

The word dating made me think of drive-in movies and old-timey saxophone music. Corny.

Paul said, "Well, I was kind of a late bloomer, you know?"

No. Not you, Paul.

"I didn't start getting out there until after high school."

If Aisha said she'd go out with me, I'd be more of a mack than Paul. I laughed a little. Couldn't help it.

"Man, you were about grown!"

Paul hung his head and laughed, then leaned back against the doorframe. I laughed at Paul laughing, then felt nervous. What if I didn't start getting girls until I was eighteen? I could be in the army by then. Or buying pornos.

We looked at each other and caught our breath, then Paul nodded into the hall and said, "Well, come eat, man."

8

We passed the mixing bowl full of spaghetti around the dinner table. In the living room, the TV flickered with the sound off, and all I could hear were forks on plates and strings of spaghetti popping into mouths. The phone rang after a minute of eating, after Uncle Paul had pointed his fork at his plate and gone, "Mmm!" but before anyone had come up for air and started really talking. Laura switched in her seat and bugged her eyes like she just knew the call was for her, but I ignored the No Phone During Meals rule and hopped up to run for it, still holding my fork.

Mama's fork banged down, "Kevin!"

"Hello?" I almost shouted into the phone. I still had some spaghetti in my mouth, and a chunk of it flew onto the stairs.

"No calls during dinner!"

Laura called out, "Take a message for me."

A small voice on the phone said, "Is Kevin there?"

I said, "Yeah," and the girl didn't say nothing. I

was 99% sure it was Aisha, but she sounded so young on the phone without her body there to drive me crazy and poke my mushy tushy, and I didn't wanna go, "This Aisha?" and have it be for Laura. Then I'd look foolish.

"That's me," I said.

"This Aisha. Calling you back."

I could hear her warm breath catching in the receiver and wanted to jump through the wires and pop out around her neck and shoulder like the phone.

"That for me?" Laura asked.

Haha, nope.

"No. Hold up."

"Hmm?" said Aisha.

"Sorry, uhh."

Aisha laughed. "What's going on?"

"I was just eating dinner."

Mama appeared in the kitchen door.

"Yes you were. Now get off the phone."

"One minute, Mama."

Aisha exhaled and shuffled.

Mama frowned and stepped back into the kitchen. I pulled the phone over to the stairs, leaned a shoulder on the wall, and spoke into my armpit.

"Uh, I called because I...do you wanna go to the movies this weekend?"

Aisha was quiet, and I planned ways to jump off

the Lee Bridge, kill Tyrell with a backhoe from the construction site on Chamberlayne, and skip school to get with Aisha in her apartment.

Then she said, "OK."

I jumped up and almost fell. When I caught myself on the railing and said, "Good," it didn't echo into the phone. I jiggled the cord and said, "Hello?" then Mama was back in the doorway, waving the other end of the phone cord. She said, "Get back to the table," right as I said, "Mama, I got a girlfriend."

The phone cord stopped and drooped over her hand, "What?"

"I was just making a date," I said.

Weren't any noises coming from the dining room. Uncle Paul and Laura were listening, and I didn't want to scream the good news anymore, so I whispered, "with a girl."

Mama looked pleased, then got serious again.

"Well, if she's so in love with you, she can wait until we get done eating."

Laura asked, "Who's in love?"

I said, "Shut up, Laura."

Uncle Paul hooted. Mama smiled, and her chest bounced, holding in a laugh.

Mama started doing the, "We don't talk on the phone during dinner. This is our family time…," speech she always gives Laura, and I thought, *Forget family time. I got a girlfriend.*

"Can't I just call her back?"

"No. Eat."

Mama pointed the phone cord toward the dining room. I walked the long way back through the living room, half high because Aisha had said yes, half in the ground because Mama had unplugged the phone. What was Aisha doing now? Dumping me for hanging up on her? Looking at her phone all confused? Paul smiled at me, and his teeth were spaghetti sauce red.

Laura said, "Baby brother got a girlfriend."

I sat down. Mama picked up her fork and started giving me sly looks. My mind went a hundred miles an hour, seeing the waving phone cord, Aisha and her orange hair talking on a purple telephone while lying on a mountain of heart-shaped, satin pillows, then spaghetti turning into a big pit of snakes curling over each other into braids. There was only one way out, and it was under the spaghetti that was getting cold in front of me.

Mama went, "Paul, just like I told you, they still ain't take the Easter decorations down."

Of course, the world had become incredible and she was still hung up on some nonsense at her job. I hung my head over my plate, stretching my mouth open as far as it would go.

Uncle Paul went, "Humph," while he was chewing, then asked, "Kevin, who's the lady?"

Laura turned at me, smiling and chewing, on "lady."

Mama stayed quiet, acting like she wasn't hopping out of her seat, waiting to hear.

I pointed my fork down at the plate and said, "Girl from school."

"School, huh?" Paul asked. Wasn't like I went much of anywhere else. When he was younger, did he know about other places to meet girls?

Enough of this talking.

I said, "Yeah," then went nuts, shoveling spaghetti into my mouth like a machine. Fork up. Spaghetti in. Chew. Fork down. Swallow while bringing up more spaghetti. Breathe.

"What's her name?"

More spaghetti in.

"Aisha," I mumbled, mouth full.

Took a drink of nasty milk. More spaghetti, working down from my chest to my stomach. Blue plate, like the spaghetti was an island that's sinking. Burp a little. Milk. Spaghetti. Answering machine clicked on by the stairs.

I was still chewing my last bite when I asked, "May I be excused?"

Everyone was looking at me. Wouldn't be a girlfriend to talk about unless I got back on that phone. Mama raised her eyebrows and looked over her glasses, like when she was pretend-offended and trying to teach manners at her school. But she said, "Yes."

I plugged the phone back in, bolted up to Mama's room, read Aisha's real number off the slip of paper, and punched it into the green buttons. The only light in the room. She answered like she'd been sitting there.

"What happened?"

"You said you'd go to the movies with me."

"Yeah, I know. Then you hung up."

"No, uh. My mama, she…" It sounded so stupid. If I was cool at all, I wouldn't have a mother who did that. "The phone's messed up. My bad."

"Oh."

"So, Saturday?" I asked.

"Sure."

She usually did most of the talking, so it was weird to be leading the conversation. I'd hoped she'd just be like, "Cool, so we'll do this, that, and the third," and I wouldn't have to scramble around hoping I didn't forget nothing like what time the flick was or if she needed a ride or if Mama drove would I sit in the back with her or if Laura would get back with Corey and he'd give us a ride but not steal Aisha from me.

"So, I…I got your number. I'll call you, and we can figure out when," I said.

"Or we could talk at school."

Word. I was about to talk, face to face, in the hall

at school, with a girl—Aisha —about going on a date.

"Yeah. Yeah. Right."

She was quiet.

I said, "Well, uh, I'll see you tomorrow."

Aisha said, "OK," and I could just hear her smiling into the phone.

I had a girlfriend. She had a boyfriend, and I was it, and my tushy wasn't really mushy, and Tyrell could just try and call me gay now.

I hung up, bounced my butt on the mattress, and pulled the shade back. The streetlights flicked on, and the evening-time houses lit up. I had a girlfriend. Now, I could enjoy the little, grown up moments where the world felt relaxed. But what to do now? They were all still eating. I might miss dessert, but Aisha's better than dessert. At least tonight. Proud as I was, I didn't want to answer a bunch of questions. I wanted the world to know about me and Aisha, but Mama ain't the world. I burped, tasted garlic powder, and felt the spaghetti tying into a knot between my chest and my belly.

CHAPTER 7: FRIDAY

1

Kevin

I came out the shower and saw Mama at her dresser, putting on makeup for her date. Before, I was kinda mad that Mama was going out with some dude, but then I started going out with Aisha, and it was like we had something to share. Was Mama going out with Earnest like they were boyfriend and girlfriend? People my age start going together and then go on dates. But old people don't do it like that. I had my towel knotted around my waist, and I sucked in my belly as I walked to Mama's door and asked, "You gettin' ready for your date?"

She stopped with some lipstick at her mouth and moved her eyes over to me. Laura had already left for her bus. It was just me and Mama having a grown folks conversation.

"Kevin, I'm going to work. I don't have a date until tonight."

Still hated hearing her say "date" though. Was Earnest gonna show up in a tux with cigarettes in the front pocket?

"You don't always put on makeup before work, though."

She already had on the slacks and smocky shirt that she wore to work, but there were a couple disco-looking outfits on the bed behind her. Nighttime clothes. Shirts with ruffles. Sleek and shiny pants. Mama doesn't dress up like that too often.

"Guess I'm just already planning. You gonna get all dressy for your date?"

Man does it suck when she says "date." Her eyes get narrow, and I swear her eyebrows are about to wiggle. Nasty. Hadn't actually thought about what I'd wear with Aisha, though.

"Probably my black hoodie, jeans."

The black hoodie's my favorite, except when I've got dandruff.

"You're not gonna dress up?"

"For the movies?!"

If she tried to get me to dress churchy for this date, I might as well stay grounded. People don't wear neckties to the goddamn movies. Even clip-on ones.

"Didn't know if you wanted to look extra nice."

She was screwing the top back on the lipstick while she talked. I don't have any nice clothes except the churchy ones. I'd love to go to Chess King and get some fly gear. New jeans. Button-up shirt. Maybe a Nautica hoodie from the department store. Whenever I wanted that stuff, Mama said I was gonna leave it somewhere or outgrow it, so I better just get some t-shirts. Didn't wanna go to the mall with Mama and Laura and get pulled into the bra section anyway. Then, I had an idea and asked, "Can I get a haircut?"

"You just got a haircut. There's no hair to cut."

"But it's growing in."

"Well, it's not grown in."

I started thinking about how much it sucks to miss the bus, even though I like the mornings when Mama gives me a ride to school. The street looks special and empty in the morning when everyone's already in school or at work.

"How'd you meet Aisha, anyway?" Mama asked.

"School."

"Yeah, I figured. Anything special happen?"

Not like we had some romantic story. I guess the mushy tushy thing was how we met, but I couldn't tell Mama that. That wasn't a story about how people got together. Guys were supposed to save girls from getting hit by cars, or win a basketball game and impress them.

"Naw, just talking in Science class."

"She good at science?"

Mama was hanging the disco clothes up in the closet. I'm not good at science.

"No, yeah, I dunno. We just talk."

"That why your grade so low?"

"No!"

Can't wait until I'm graduated and don't have her asking about grades. By then, I'll have so many girlfriends it won't even be a thing when I go on a date.

"OK, OK. Well, I hope you have fun."

"Uh, hope you do, too. Mama, you gonna be home to make us dinner tonight?"

She shut the closet door and said, "Yes, Kevin."

"What we having?"

"I don't know."

"Can I be in charge tonight when you go out?"

I couldn't say, "on your date."

Laura was usually in charge, but things were different now that I was going out with a girl, and I'm a teenager. Plus, if I was in charge, I could make Laura do the dishes.

"You'll both be in charge, but your sister's still mainly in charge. She's older. When I know I can trust you both enough to—"

"Alright, alright," I said. Suddenly, I remembered all the stuff I had to do before my bus. Couldn't wait to bounce along on the seat, knowing I was going out with somebody. Maybe I'd joke with the eighth graders.

2

David was standing under the tree with his back to me, watching for the bus. Geek. I was glad I'd gotten a girl before David, because I worry that hanging out with him will make me a geek, too. But going out with Aisha proved that I wasn't meant to spend my life on the block with him. It would have really messed things up if David was touching titties first. Can't wait to touch titties. I walked up. I'd been waiting for so long to be able to tell David I had a girlfriend. Maybe now I could hook him up, because I'd know more girls. We could all get it on at his place. His mama's never there.

It's the friend's job to get the word out. How does it usually spread? I'm used to seeing couples talking in the hall one day, then by lunch the next day, everyone in school knows how far they'd gone under the bleachers, or in the bathroom of the sub shop on Brook Rd. Sometimes, Demetric tells me during class, "Shawnelle went in the janitor shed with two of those Gilpin Court niggas after school." Or a loud girl is chanting the news in the hall, "Tameka went to second with Eric, right behind Starlina's back." But how does it start? Someone has to tell someone else. I was cheesing as David turned around. Couldn't help myself.

"We still gonna go see... Man, what you standing there grinning for?" David said.

"I'm goin' out with Aisha."

Aisha, that I think about every day, stare at, dream about, imagining her apartment and running my fingers across the back of her hand.

"How you gonna be going out with someone if you're grounded?"

I quit cheesing. That's why David will never get any. He doesn't understand. Leaves rustled, and a bird flew out the tree above us.

"Called her. We're going to the movies this weekend."

I was cheesing again. Breeze on my teeth.

David frowned and raised a hand, "But we're going to the movies this weekend."

Dang.

"David, man, look, we gotta go see *The Mask* next weekend."

David's hand stayed up.

I said, "Or maybe one day after school?"

The hand went down. I felt bad, but if he doesn't understand why this is a big deal, then he really is never gonna get any.

I wished Aisha was in my lunch, so I could sit with her. But if she was, she'd have to sit with David, and that would be wack as all get-out. Aisha sitting like four feet away from David while he dribbles chocolate milk down his shirt. What happens to people's friends when they start going out with other people? I guess the friends just wait until they're not going out anymore.

A pit bull, chained in a yard up the block, started barking and shaking the fence.

David finally said, "Alright, man. Alright."

But I could tell it wasn't alright. The David that had punched me in the cafeteria was a new David, and I didn't want to see him again.

"Dawg, I'm sorry. I just…" I chuckled and felt cool to be able to say it, "I just gotta go on this date."

My world was different. I was going out with somebody. My tushy wasn't mushy. Maybe I could use Uncle Paul's weights, so my chest would be pumped when Aisha took my shirt off. The bus came, and David sat there looking out the window, so I sat across the aisle, propped against the window with an arm down the back of my seat like I was in a hot tub.

At school, Demetric was walking with these two other guys. I clapped him on the shoulder and said, "Yo, D."

His friends had no expressions. They could be about to stomp me or bust out laughing. Usually, I wouldn't have gone up, but I had some news.

Demetric said, "Waddup, K.?"

"I'm going out with Aisha, yo."

I lifted a hand for five.

He said, "Oh yeah? Since when?"

Why was he playing it so cool?

"Last night. We talked…on the phone."

One of Demetric's boys snickered. I screwfaced him. Demetric finally hit me with a thumb-lock five.

3

In the cafeteria, I always walk fast by the project girls' table, and they always ignore me and keep having that type of fun that looks like it's about to be a fight. This time though, Tameka was on her knee on her seat, leaning over the table with her booty pointed into the aisle. I had my eyes down, but the booty was level with my lunch tray and heart-shaped in black jeans, like a pillow I'd want on my couch. Tameka must have felt my eyes, so she turned and stood with jeans pushing up her belly so she looked like an ice cream cone. Not my type of ice cream! I saw her watching me and kept moving in case she tried to play snatchies on my tray.

Tameka moved her hips right, then switched them left and asked, "You goin' out with Aisha?"

The girls on either side of her spun out to watch over their shoulders, and the cafeteria lights made shiny, white squares on their lotioned-up foreheads. I said, "Yeah," loud enough for them all to hear, then broke out cheesing again. Even my lunch tray felt cool in my hands. Tameka stood there. Her friends looked at one another, and I heard trays banging onto tables around me, people giving each other five and dropping their bookbags to eat.

"You know she went to third with that nigga Dwayne who go to John Marshall."

Who's this Dwayne? A high school guy?! Probably has a mustache. Probably lives in her apartment complex.

I said, "Oh."

"Haha, yeah," Tameka said, skipping sideways with her mouth open, so damn happy to have messed up my day. Her friends started snickering. I squeezed my lunch tray extra hard and went to find David.

Still hadn't seen Aisha. Third base or not, I couldn't wait to go to her in the hall and put my arm around her. How long did it take Dwayne to get to third? Would me and Aisha go out that long?

4

All day between classes, I'd been getting sidelong glances from people who were in on the news, but I didn't see Aisha until before last period. I'd borrowed a Certs from this dude in math class, then I ate it right away. I knew that me and Aisha usually passed each other in the west hall, where they haven't painted in a while, and it still looks like the 1970s with brown floor tiles and pea green lockers with dark wood trim. She was amazing standing at her locker. Her orange hair was exotic fish bright in the sun from the high-up windows, and her purple jeans looked like old school graffiti against the green lockers. Shadows made her eyes bigger, and she moved in slow motion. Ducking into her locker to fish out a book. Leaning back and slamming the door. Turning to face me. Me not even smiling, just nodding slow as I walked up to her. The rule is to always walk on the right side of the hall, but I cut across, hopping fast, so I wouldn't bump into these two guys in polos. One of them sucked his teeth and went, "Dang," when I passed too close. Then, I could see her again, facing me and breathing out of her puffy cheeks, gold love glowing inside her locker. I felt floaty and thought my toes could wiggle and make me fly. I expected my arms to reach out and grab her, but they stayed at my sides. I didn't know what to do with them. Wished I was holding a basketball or something. She lifted her blue bookbag onto one shoulder. I walked up and said, "Hey," right as she said, "Did you tell Demetric we were going out?"

I said, "Yeah."

It sounded like a question. I touched the crinkly windbreaker on her right shoulder.

ZERO FADE

She looked down at it and asked, "Since when are we going out?"

"Since we talked last night."

She breathed deep, got taller, then sagged again, and I got ready to catch her. The people passing by were trying to beat the bell, so they didn't notice me touching a girl.

"Kevin. I said I'd go to the movies with you."

"I know!"

My arm was starting to get tired.

"That doesn't mean we're going out."

"Oh."

I dropped my hand to my side and scratched the seam of my jeans. I got quiet and tried to make my question sound like a good idea, not begging. It didn't work.

I asked, "Do you want to be going out?"

She looked away and fiddled with her backpack strap.

"I don't know."

I had a fist in my throat. What was I gonna tell Mama and Uncle Paul and Laura and David and people at school? She looked back at me, so I asked, "Do you still want to go to the movies on Saturday?"

She looked back down. I traced her hair down to her scalp with my eyes until she said, "I can't."

"Oh."

"A'ight?"

"A'ight."

No, it wasn't "A'ight," but I couldn't say that. Couldn't tell her how it felt to be back at the bottom, back to not going out with anyone, back to being like David. Maybe David still wanted to catch *The Mask* on Saturday.

"Well, I gotta go to class," Aisha said.

I said, "OK," because I figured if I was nice, she might change her mind sometime. It was hard.

She got on her tiptoes, put her arms around my neck, and hugged me. Her hair went in my nose, and it smelled like burnt toast and peach shampoo. Think I felt her chest pressing into me under the windbreaker. I clapped my hands onto her bookbag and squeezed a textbook. It felt like what I'd wanted all this time, but it hurt, because now I knew what it was like, and I might never get it again.

She said, "See you in Science," and pulled back so my hands dropped.

I stared at her locker and thought of the things I'd wanted to leave in there. Notes. Songs. Gifts that would fit through the little vents. If I could think of that for her, maybe I'd think of it for someone else. But I wanted it to be her. The hall was empty. Aisha walked away, trailing a hand along the lockers to her right, a sunbeam giving her a halo of dust.

I tried to rush to class, but my breath got heavy, my eyes squinted, and I was scared I'd cry. I barely beat the bell and had to sit in the front row by the skinny nerds and churchy kids. In my head, there was a big, black space behind me, and I pretended that rumors never started. That girls never changed their minds. If she really couldn't go out Saturday, she would have said so last night. She was lying to avoid me. That's how wack I am.

5

After school, I watched TV, waiting for an excuse to change the channel. I'd already been through the rotation twice. Wasn't nothing on at four on a Friday afternoon, because everyone who was cool had something to do. Except me, stuck in on my last day of punishment.

I would have snuck over to David's and watched cable, maybe *American Gladiators*, or something on MTV that made it feel like the weekend was what everyone was waiting for, even though the people watching were sitting around with no ideas. Plus, David was pissed at me for ditching him. The way things were going, he probably had a date with Aisha.

No *Mask*. No date. No Aisha at all. Might as well stay grounded. Laura's key turned in the lock, then the door creaked open.

"Yo," I said.

"Yo," she said, underhanding her keys onto the telephone table.

I hadn't looked at the phone book. Maybe someone else was looking at Aisha's number. Who else could like her? She's mine.

"You ever tried to stay grounded for longer, so you won't get grounded the next time?"

Laura stopped kicking off her sneakers and looked at me like I was nuts.

"What?"

"See, I'm grounded—"

"Yeah, no kiddin'," she said, and dropped her bookbag at the bottom of the stairs.

"Tomorrow, I'm off being grounded. But I don't got nothing to do. I figured I could stay grounded longer to save up for the next time I..."

It sounded stupid once I said it out loud. Laura shook her head and dropped into the armchair at the head of the couch.

"Thought you were gonna go out with... Aaaisha," she said, wiggling her eyebrows.

I put my feet on the coffee table, looked at them and said, "She can't."

Laura straightened her back and asked, "She can't?"

"No."

Laura stayed quiet for a minute. Over the tops of my shoes, I could tell she was looking at me like she was sorry. Made me feel worse, stupid for having to get sympathy. She stood up, looked in the mirror over the fireplace and said, "Imma get a soda. You want a soda?"

"Yeah."

She came back a minute later with two cans of Richfood black cherry. I was watching a minivan commercial.

"What happened with this girl?"

"She said just 'cos we were gonna go out this weekend didn't mean we were *going out*, then she said she couldn't go to the movies."

I sounded whiny. It's embarrassing when you think something's going to be perfect, and it turns into a mess.

"That's wack," Laura said, burping into the back of her hand and setting the soda on the coffee table.

"Yeah. It's wack! She's wack! Leavin' me with nothing to do."

Laura turned away. Maybe she was laughing, but I didn't say nothing, because talking mess made me feel better. You can ground me for popping off at the mouth, but I still love to do it.

"Why don't you kick it with David?" Laura asked.

Ugh. I leaned back on the couch and told the ceiling, "He pissed at me."

"That little squirt is mad?"

"We were gonna go see *The Mask*. Then, I told him

I had a date and couldn't go. And he said I just use him for his cable."

And now I don't have a date. Took a swig of soda. Bubbles on my tongue.

"Whatever," Laura said.

"Yeah. Whatever."

"*The Mask* look funny, too. I'll go. You wanna go tomorrow?" Laura asked.

"You like *The Mask*?" I was still holding my soda by my mouth, and my voice buzzed in the can.

"Yeah," Laura was nodding. "That Fire Marshall Bill dude funny."

We both said, "Let me show ya something," like Fire Marshall Bill, and I started to cool down.

"When Mama get home, I'll tell her I want to go with you. But you gotta promise you won't try and hold my hand in the movie. I ain't your date."

6

I fuss about how the weekend is boring, but one good thing is that, every Friday, we have a family dinner and either get takeout pizza or Chinese, or Mama makes something good like tacos or chicken. Tacos are my favorite. I put on extra cheese until it snows out the butt end when I bite into it. The door opened downstairs, and my stomach started asking me questions, but Mama gets salty when I bother her as soon as she walks in, so I played it cool until I smelled onions frying downstairs.

I followed the scent and found Mama in baby blue sweatpants, working the knife through a tomato so that little red cubes fell away every time the blade ticked on our old, wood cutting board. I like that cutting board, I like Mama, and I knew what was coming.

"You're smart Kevin, but sometimes you gotta think before you talk."

She used the knife to scrape the tomato into a pile, then started cutting long slices in a stack of crisp lettuce leaves. We always have a conversation like this at the end of punishment. It reminds me of after a basketball game, when the announcers talk about the highlights. Instead of a replay of someone dunking, it'd be slo-mo of Mama chasing me out the basement. That was kinda funny.

I bit my lip and said, "Yes ma'am."

"Don't 'ma'am' me. This ain't the army. You sound fake as all get-out, Kevin."

Mama was talking in that fake-joking way she uses when she's trying to make a point without being pushy. It's wack, but I wasn't gonna say nothing. She turned, dropped a brick of pink ground beef into the skillet with the onions and scattered it with the spatula.

What is fake? If I speak my mind, I get in trouble,

and if I try to be nice, it doesn't work. I opened my mouth to say something I hadn't thought of yet, then thought better of thinking of anything and closed it again. Mama turned back and the knife crunched through the lettuce, then stopped.

"You know, you haven't said sorry yet."

Her voice sounded sad now. I was sorry for calling Mama "fat," but I don't like saying sorry. Talk about fake. People act like you can do whatever, then make it OK by saying sorry. Like, if Tyrell said, "I'm sorry," for throwing a basketball at me in gym class, I still wouldn't like him. And if I was really sorry, I wouldn't have popped off at Mama in the first place.

But I did feel bad. Mama's not really fat. Sure, she don't look like Nia Long or nothing, but that's for the better. Having a sexy mama would be confusing as hell. I watched Mama cooking with sureness, like the back of her brain had taken over, turning from the counter to the stove to move the ground beef around in the pan. She's alright in my book. Sure, she grounds me, but she makes tacos.

I told her back, "Sorry Mama. I shouldn'ta said that."

She didn't move. The greasy spatula shined in the air over the skillet.

"It's alright, baby. Thank you."

During dinner, Laura kept buddying up to Mama and asking what time she was gonna get back.

"I dunno," Mama said, clinking her fork down on the plate. "After the concert. I ain't the O'Jays. I don't know what time they'll stop."

It was funny for a couple reasons. One, because Mama and Laura have the same conversation whenever Laura's about to go out, but then it's Laura saying, "Out," when Mama asks her where she's going. And then it's Mama being like, "You are home at 11. Curfew in this house is 11. And now, thanks to all those little n-words out shooting guns and selling crack, the curfew in the city is 11. And I ain't getting outta bed to bail you out if you get caught playing around after 11. I need my beauty sleep before I go to the police station, because I can't be out there looking like that trash."

Laura always listens and rolls her eyes. I roll my eyes, too, because I've heard it so many times. Once, I was calling Laura into my room to hear a song on the radio, and she shouted, "I can't be out there looking like that trash," across the hall. Mama was in her room and laughed. Now, when Mama gets to the end of her sermon about curfew, we all smile when she says, "I can't be out there looking like that trash."

The other thing that was funny about Laura giving

Mama the third degree was that Laura only asked so she'd know if she could stay out late. But Mama never told her. She just came downstairs all shiny with lipstick and nice shoes and left a trail of perfume to the backdoor like a little boat through water. Car cut on a minute later, like Mama clearing her throat. Guess Earnest doesn't have a car.

Five minutes later, I'm watching TV and hear the front door unlatch behind me. It's Laura walking out, so I hop up and say, "Wait, let me get my shoes," and she just goes, "Psssh," and slams the door behind her. The lock clicks, and it's just like earlier—me and the TV and nothing else doing.

Wish I could tell you that when I opened the fridge for a soda a whole party, with a DJ and some fine women in fishnets, tumbled out into the kitchen, and I got laid and joined a rap group, but really I just kept feeling low. Low because Friday night was happening even for Mama, and there I was pretending it was Tuesday. Low because no Aisha tomorrow, or ever. But also kinda a'ight about that because it meant I didn't have to spend the night doing twenty pushups, then twenty sit-ups, then twenty pushups to get my front up like I'd promised myself. None of that. Low because I didn't know what David was doing, but it was for sure that he thought he was too good to be doing it with me, and that wasn't how things were supposed to go down. TV was wack. Couple reruns on. I fell asleep in the chair and woke up to the creaky sound of the door opening. My mouth had that dry taste that I always imagine Egyptian mummies smell like, and I blinked slow to wet my eyes and looked over. Mama was inching through the doorway butt-first, catching the iron storm door with her hand so it wouldn't slam. She shut it, and when she saw me watching her, she jumped a bit and broke out smiling.

"Hi Mama."

"Hi Kevin."

She looked down at her purse, and when she looked up, she was still smiling.

"You had fun?"

She walked slow like her heels were hurting her and set her purse on the phone table.

"I did."

"Cool."

I started to smile, too. I expected it to be nasty to see Mama coming home happy, but it was kinda nice.

"You getting excited for tomorrow?"

I wished she was talking about punishment ending, but I knew she meant my date.

"She can't go."

"What?" Mama stood by the table with both hands taking off her left earring.

"She said she can't go."

"Why, baby?"

"I dunno. She just can't."

Couldn't tell Mama I'd been wrong in the first place, because then she'd start talking about how I had to be on top of things more.

"You gonna go out with Earnest again?"

"Maybe," she smiled, kinda embarrassed, and reached for her right earring. "I had fun. But I just got done going out with him once."

Man. Grown folks do it different. But, I bet Mama and Earnest don't walk around the church basement with their arms around each other, and that's good. Right then, the phone rang and Mama turned to answer. I slipped by her up the stairs and heard her saying, "Yes, Laura. It's me. In the flesh. And your curfew is still 11."

CHAPTER 8: NEXT SATURDAY

1

Kevin

I woke up to the smell of smoky bacon filling the house. When Mama cooks bacon, you rub the smell into your face after you shower because it lingers in the towels. I smiled and heard laughing downstairs—Mama and Uncle Paul. Everyone was happy. I was done being grounded and was about to see *The Mask*. I'd asked out a girl, she'd sort of said yes, then no, so it was like I'd already had a girlfriend. Felt good to have that out the way.

A slice of sun shot through the curtain and across my bed. I pressed my shoulders into the mattress and stretched my chest towards the ceiling. Saturday was mine, and I wanted to roar like a lion. No homework 'til tomorrow. No explaining about

Aisha to Demetric 'til Monday.

More laughing. Uncle Paul getting musical like he does when he loses himself talking to Mama. They were probably talking about Mama's date. What was it like? Mama and a bunch of old people getting down at a concert. Mama doing the weird, high laugh she does when she's on the phone with work people. Mama getting kissed on? Nasty. The sun was hot. I pushed my blanket aside and went into the bathroom.

2

Paul

Downstairs, Sheila pulled wavy slices of bacon from the skillet and placed them on a folded paper towel.

"Paul is seeing someone special today," she sang.

Paul was dressed a little nicer. Wine-colored turtleneck. Clean, black jeans. Shined, black, low top boots. Goatee trimmed. He patted the air in front of him and said, "Keep it down, keep it down."

"Hey now, you don't want the whole world to know?" Sheila asked, dumping a mixing bowl of eggs into the skillet.

"Well, I don't know if the whole world," Paul said, pointing to the ceiling, "is ready to know."

Sheila nodded and began scrambling the eggs.

Paul kept his voice quiet, mingling it with the spatula's scrape on the skillet, the toaster's ding.

"Couple days back, that boy asked me if his haircut looked gay. Was all worked up."

"Hmm," Sheila said, staring into the pan. Paul watched her shoulder pump while she cooked.

"What do you think?" Paul asked.

Sheila shook her head and said, "He's young."

"Not too young to be saying some things, though."

What was the worst thing that would happen if Kevin found out? He wouldn't do something ridiculous like fight him, but things might never be the same. Paul had seen that happen before. The friends who wouldn't ride in the car with him, who were sure to take an armchair if he was on the couch, who looked at him with suspicion when a muscular man passed by. Paul wasn't even that into muscles. It hurt. It was like being gay made him suddenly untrustworthy, like it deleted every good thing he'd ever done as a friend. He didn't want that to happen with his nephew.

What would Kevin say? It wouldn't be anything new, but it would hurt more. It's one thing for a drunk man to stumble into the wrong bar and spit insults, because that drunk man is gone within seconds. But, your family doesn't go away, no matter how hard you wish. Paul sighed into his coffee cup, thinking of the conversations that he stopped having with his own father.

But it would be worse to not tell the kid, and have

him figure it out on his own later. Then it'd be like Paul had been lying this whole time. He was sick of that feeling.

Sheila shrugged and said, "I could tell him."

"No," Paul dismissed the easy out. "It should be from me." He took a sip of coffee. It went down hard, and the back of his throat tingled with new saliva. The toaster dinged.

"Would you butter that?" Sheila asked. "When do you think you're gonna say something?"

"Maybe I should tell him at breakfast."

Paul stood and used a finger to flick each slice of bread out of the toaster oven and into a stack on a plate. It had gone easy with Laura. She'd asked Sheila. And women don't get as upset by these things as men. Some women were relieved to find out, because then they knew that he wouldn't make a pass. For men, it was the opposite.

"Let that boy eat first," Sheila said.

Brother and sister laughed.

"I'm getting tired of this, though," Paul said, then sat down and squished a piece of bread with the butter knife.

Sheila turned, "What else has he been saying?"

"Nothing. I'm just... I'm sick of feeling like two people. Like I've gotta hide what feels right to me. Like I can only act the way that I need to every now and then."

Paul stared into the yellow tub of margarine.

"Kevin needs to know. The other day I came home to him dressed up in all red, pretending to be Eddie Murphy, and mouthing along with *Delirious*."

Paul put his forehead in his hand, and the table wobbled while he chuckled. "No kidding."

Sheila laughed at the memory. "I asked him if he ever played that Eddie Murphy tape with you, and he got all excited that you might like it too."

"Well, I do."

It took Paul a minute to remember all of the faggot jokes on that album. Thing was, he heard foolish mess like that and didn't always connect it to himself. Eddie was funny and something else on the long list of things that Paul liked, but that might not like him. Eddie always seemed kinda suspect, though. A little too smiley in that tight, red leather.

"He just has no idea about why some of those Eddie Murphy jokes might bother people."

"Hmm, I bet." Paul shook his head. "Speaking of botherin', how'd that date go last night?"

Sheila focused all of her attention on lowering the flame under the eggs. Paul smiled over his coffee until she said, "It went. It sure did. O'Jays still got their moves."

Paul didn't miss a beat. Grinning, he said, "This Earnest got moves, too?"

Sheila laughed and switched her butt to an

imagined beat. "Oh, we did some dancing. But I go out for fun, and my mind's on things at home."

Paul wished he cared that much about something.

3
Kevin

I was sitting across from Mama. Mama, who just went on a date. Uncle Paul came in from the kitchen with the plate of toast and some slick clothes on and said, "Big K!"

He had that great smile that made me want to smile too, and I stopped being embarrassed about Aisha and said, "Sup!" then used my fork to take three pieces of bacon off the plate in the middle of the table, even though Mama looks at me sideways if I take more than two.

Uncle Paul stood over Mama and started clowning, talking in a real formal voice, "Oh, big sister. Would you care for some toast?"

People treating Mama special now that she went on a date. Next to me, steam puffed up as Laura took the plate off the bowl of eggs and started serving herself. She asked, "How was it, Mama?"

"It was fun," Mama answered, looking embarrassed, which made her seem younger. "Gimme that bread, boy!"

She grabbed the plate from Uncle Paul, who put his hands on his hips and said, "You avoiding the question, big sister? The lady Laura wants to know how your date went."

I wished they were asking me these questions tomorrow after I'd went out with Aisha. I'd be like, "It was cool," but in my head, I'd be thinking, "I got to second." Did Mama go to second? Nasty.

Laura's fork clinked on her plate. I saw three slices of bacon on Uncle Paul's plate, too. Mama said, "It was nice. I wanna find a concert I can take you guys to sometime."

I smiled and said, "Redman," before imagining Mama with her hood up, holding a 40 and throwing elbows thug-style at a rap concert. Wanted to go to a concert, though.

"Well, we'll see," Mama said. "I looked in the paper. That *Mask* movie is playing at 12:05."

Laura said, "Cool."

Mama asked, "You wanna go, too?"

"Yeah."

I was glad Laura wasn't saying nothing about how she was standing in as my date. Then, Uncle Paul asked, "You still taking out that girl from school?"

He looked excited for me. Glad I wasn't a late bloomer like him. And that made it even worse that I'd have to tell him. I didn't say nothing for a second, then Mama opened her mouth, and I knew I'd have to say something before she embarrassed me.

"She can't," I said.

Paul set his fork down. "She can't?"

I started to get brave. "No, man. Damn."

I shook my head and looked at my plate. Paul said, "I'm sorry to hear that, man."

I raised my head and caught him and Mama shooting each other a look. They laughing at me? I frowned. Laura said, "Don't you worry, K. I'll tell her what's what next I see her."

I didn't want Laura hitting Aisha with her purse. I wanted Aisha to go out with me and sit by me at the flicks this afternoon instead of my sister. Instead of David. I threw some eggs in my mouth and said, "It's cool," before I chewed them. A little bit of egg fell back out onto my plate.

"Manners like that, you might need a little practice before you start going on dates," Mama said, and I got heated and pointed my fork at her, ready to say a thing or two. Uncle Paul cut me off with a hand and said, "Sheila, let the man be. It ain't easy out there. Gonna be some time before he starts taking ladies to concerts like some people here."

He patted her shoulder. Mama made that embarrassed smile again. I was like, *No. I'm gonna get some girls before I'm old as dirt like Mama.* Didn't say that though. Said, "Uncle Paul, you said you didn't start going out with girls until after high school?"

Same look between Uncle Paul and Mama again. Not laughing at me. Serious stuff. Laura looked up, then Uncle Paul said, "Actually, Kevin. It took me a while to get out there. I had a girlfriend for a little bit in high school, but..." Paul paused and looked over my shoulder, into the kitchen. "What I meant the other day was that I didn't really start dating until after I graduated."

I folded half a piece of toast into my mouth. Only one girlfriend? After he graduated? Does he mean he stayed a virgin that long? Don't let that happen to me!

I asked, "Really?" My voice squeaked with surprise and everyone laughed, so I said, "But, you're the man, Uncle Paul. How were the ladies not going crazy for you?"

Quiet again. Mama scraped some eggs into a careful pile with her fork. Uncle Paul sighed and looked at the plate of toast.

"K. That wasn't exactly the problem. It was more that..." he looked at the corner of the ceiling, then at my ear, "I wasn't going crazy for the ladies."

Wonder what the hell else he did in middle school then. I asked, "You were a late bloomer?"

Hate that word. It's a nice thing that people call losers. Don't want any late bloomers in my family. Then, I might be one too. Dang. I gotta have more than one girlfriend in high school. Gotta have two or three every year, then, when I'm a junior, I'll get my license and a car and go out with a girl all year so we can do it.

"K. Look man. Something I've been wanting to tell you," Uncle Paul said, looking right at me, all serious, eyes kinda buggy behind his glasses. "I don't like ladies like that. There are some fine ladies out there, for sure. But, I like men."

"You like men?"

It took me a second to get it. Uncle Paul was looking at me, raising his head in the slowest nod in the world. I was watching his eyes. Same eyes I'd seen before, but they were different, on a person I didn't know. What nasty things had those eyes looked at?

"So, then, you like gay dudes?"

Mama said, "Kevin," in a warning voice, and Laura made a quick, "Hmph," next to me, but I had to know. Gay dudes are like that one guy with the toothy, fake smile who walks his little dog by the park, or the white guy with the flowery sport shirts who comes to school to work with the retards. They get clowned. People don't clown Uncle Paul. Better not.

"Well, uh... Kevin. I like who I like. And I like you, you're part of my fam—"

I yelled, "I ain't gay!"

Pushed my plate away and my chair screeched back. I turned heel and busted through the kitchen to the stairs. Smelled like cooking in the kitchen, and my stomach was doing flips, still hungry, but sick. All this time, I was worried about that barber and really I'd been kicking it with a gay dude since I was a baby. Did people know and look at me strange? Had I been learning gay things from Uncle Paul by accident? Was that why Aisha wouldn't go to the movies and Tyrell was always tripping?

I went in the bathroom. The whole world was different. I might as well piss in the tub and wash up in the toilet. I looked in the mirror and read the backwards labels on the shelf behind me.

eniretsiL.

lohoclA.

Now, I knew I wouldn't go to the movie. It's OK, though. I couldn't sit in the theater with images of Uncle Paul kissing dudes bouncing in the dark in front of me.

etagloC.

I cupped my hands full of sink water and splashed my head to cool down. Little rivers ran down the stubble from last week's fade. The fade my gay uncle had took me to get from one of his gay friends. Was everyone else in that barbershop gay? I couldn't tell anymore. I touched the stubble. It was getting soft. Maybe I could go to a different barber next time, but with who?

nimrahC.

I really hated my pop for leaving me with my nasty,

gay uncle. I crossed to my room. It was sunny, golden, and warm, and it smelled like a sleepy bed. I sat there just like last Saturday, counting down until I was back on punishment. I don't want to be a late bloomer, but how can I get my life to start if I'm grounded, back-to-back, until I'm eighteen?

I heard feet on the stairs and got worried it was Mama, but then I recognized Uncle Paul's footsteps. I know him so good, I know his steps. What's worse? Getting grounded or having to talk to your gay uncle? I squeezed the edge of my mattress until Uncle Paul showed up, holding my plate, thumb clamping down my fork, black specks from all the pepper I'd put on my eggs and an extra piece of bacon. Everyone likes bacon. Even faggots.

"I brought you this," Uncle Paul said, lifting the plate. Sun glinted on the bacon grease. I just watched him. He put the plate on my dresser and said, "Look. I know it might take a while to sink in. But remember, we're still family. I still," he paused, "love you like I did before."

Nasty.

There were about a hundred things I wanted to ask—When did Paul turn gay? Does Paul act different with me than he does with gay guys? Had I looked gay in the car with him? Could an uncle be gay for his nephew? Did Uncle Paul have a boyfriend?—but I couldn't think of nothing to say.

"I'm still the same guy," Uncle Paul said. "Is it that bad?"

He stood near me with the Uncle Paul smell, a little cologne and the sandalwood from his jacket. It smelled good. Was that a gay smell?

"Why'd you lie to me?" I asked.

"Lie to you?"

"All this time not telling, it's like a lie. Why ain't you warned me?"

"Warned you?"

"Yeah. That you gay. So I..."

So I could what? Not sure. But it was like he'd been lying to me this whole time, and I thought I knew him, and he was the man, but there he went, getting it on with dudes.

"So you what, Kevin? I'm still your uncle."

"And you still a nasty faggot."

Uncle Paul made fists, and I leaned back, but he turned around and walked out the room. And there I was, alone again, waiting for Mama to come tell me not to bother making plans.

4

I put on a tape, quiet, so maybe Mama would forget about me. The door creaked open downstairs, and Uncle Paul didn't sound gay when he said, "Goodbye." A minute later, Mama was at my door in her stupid,

223

green plaid bedroom slippers. She still had on a little makeup from last night.

"You call David yet?" she asked.

"No, I…" I caught myself before I said, "thought I was grounded."

"Well, we got some talkin' to do first. But, I still want you out of the house this afternoon. I've had enough of you around here. And besides, if you get out more, you'll be exposed to more things."

"Like the movie?"

The pipes groaned and water splashed as Laura started the shower.

"No. I just mean that you can get out and be around more people."

Sounded good to me. Wish Aisha was one of those people.

"But, you never know, might be some scary," Mama shook her hands like a haunted house monster, "homosexuals at the mall. You'll have to look out."

She thinks she's so damn funny. I shifted on the bed. Mama said, "You can't talk to your uncle, or anyone, like that."

"Why ain't he told me?"

Mama walked up to the boombox and spun the radio tuner, then said, "Turn off that GD tape."

When I leaned over, Mama sat down, and the mattress bucked so I almost flew off. Closest I've come to being in bed with a woman and it's Mama.

Nasty. Coulda been Aisha. Did Mama get in bed with Earnest last night? Extra nasty. Everything nasty. I asked Mama again, "Why ain't he told me?"

Mama sighed. Her glasses glinted in the sun and she said, "Why *didn't* he *tell* you?"

There she goes with that grammar. I didn't roll my eyes, though. Didn't want her to change her mind. She said, "He was looking for the right time. I guess he was scared of what you'd think."

Since when do grown folks care what kids think? I didn't even believe it when I was saying, "He was scared?"

"That man cares about you, Kevin."

Grown folks say they care about you when they're trying to keep you from having fun. I have to stay in and do homework because Mama cares. I can't kick it in Battery Park at night because the guys there are "hoodlums," and Mama cares. If Uncle Paul cared, what was that keeping me from doing?

"Why's he have to be gay?" I asked.

Mama shifted, and the bed bounced.

"That's not for me to know, but I will say, he's been like that for a long time, and knowing has made him happier."

"How?"

"It's who he really is."

This wasn't making sense. Gay dudes are sissies, and Uncle Paul is definitely not a sissy. So, what was he really? Mama kept going.

"And he's still my brother, and you're still gonna see a lot of him, so you'd better get used to it."

This was true. I folded my hands together and nodded. Wasn't like Uncle Paul was gonna disappear through a sparkly, pink door in the sky. Mama asked, "You gonna act all weird next time he comes over?"

Being mad isn't acting weird. How else could I act around Uncle Paul now? We couldn't go nowhere together. I sure wasn't gonna tell nobody about him being gay, but still, people must know. Bit my lip. Didn't want to spoil not being grounded. How could things be the same with Uncle Paul? I smelled Laura's fruity shampoo and reached for the plate on my dresser. I could go for some OJ. "No. I'll be cool," I said.

"Cool," Mama said, then smiled to herself. "Some words never go out of style. Cool." She stood up and I almost fell over again. She stopped in the door, "Tell David to get over here at 11:30."

It was raining a little, so the car tires made sizzling sounds in the street. Laura was up front, and I shut my ears when she started asking Mama about her date. Just kept picturing Mama at the prom, or Mama doing the things people at school talk about. Nasty. David was by me, wearing the shiny blue raincoat he'd had since fifth grade and a big, geeky watch that he frowned down at every few seconds.

David had that Grandma's house smell that he gets when he stays over there while his Mama's out. Mothballs and oil burning in the pan. I sniffed over at him and said, "Pancakes?"

David jerked his arm back and went, "Shut up. Yeah."

"Hey man, 'Sssmokin'!'"

David looked me in the eye all serious and said, "How good is this gonna be?"

He was leaning across the seat so close I thought he was gonna kiss me. Did he know about Uncle Paul? He smelled like old lady soap. I put my head on the cool window and got a little mad that, instead of Aisha, I was in the car with David, who thought that Biggie Smalls was one of the Cosby Kids. We rolled up to a green light and Mama had to brake because the Jeep in front of us slowed down, thinking we were an unmarked cop car.

5

People were shadows in their cars, hissing through the mall lot. I got excited when I saw the ticket line through the tall movie theater windows. It was all people who don't live on Hanes Ave. or go to Henderson. I might go to high school with some of them. One could be my girlfriend. They might laugh at my jokes.

Mama stopped, and I hopped out while David was playing with his seatbelt. The quicker I got away from the car, the less of a chance someone would see Mama's sweatpants and say something.

I got in line and David caught up, then edged in front of me, looking at his watch again. Laura showed up on the other side of the red velvet rope, back to the windows. She grabbed inside my elbow and said, "Come on y'all," looking to David and jerking her head at the door.

I pulled my arm back. What was she doing?

She said, "Let's go," and I thought of the times we'd gone to the mall and she'd ditched me to hang out with the high school kids who smoke by the food court. She wished I'd go away back then, but since she was asking me to go, I knew it wouldn't be like that.

I ducked under the rope and out of line. David bugged his eyes and stuck out his left hand and my heart sank. Jim Carrey in green face paint and a crazy suit popped into my head. I wanted to see the movie. But I also wanted to kick it with Laura. I wanted to stop watching the people in the movies make jokes and go make my own.

"David. Now we got some time to go to the mall," I said.

I tried to make it sound exciting and like it wasn't a surprise to me too, but I knew David didn't care about the mall. He didn't wanna look at girls or the new British Knights. He just wanted to see *The Mask*.

"Where are you going, Kevin? We're supposed to see this movie!"

He sounded like a baby, but he was right. Laura shifted on her feet, about to run off without me. I lifted the rope, then this girl with fingerwaves said, "Why you trying to cut?" Laura popped her neck at the loudmouth, then turned to me with the same type of mean-mug and said, "Let's go, Kevin. Train's leavin'."

"Train's leavin'" is one of Mama's expressions. My insides were hopping. The line moved. David went with it, and I walked with him, skimming my hand on the dusty rope. Laura took a step back.

I said, "What do you say, D? I say we hit the mall."

David shifted on his feet like a video game boxer and said, "What do I say? I say we see *The Mask* like we've been talking about doing all week. And you don't get yourself put on punishment again."

Behind us, Fingerwaves did one of those "Ha-HAAA!" laughs like Tyrell's boys. Laura glared from her to me.

David said, "What are you gonna do at the mall, anyway?"

I didn't know, but I needed to find out. Me and David could kick it any day, but Laura was older and did stuff besides play Sega Genesis or shoot baskets if the high school guys weren't on the court.

The line moved up again. Laura turned to the

door. My heart started rushing. I checked the lot for Mama's car, then turned to David and said, "I'll meet you at the bus stop after the movie."

David stuck his hand out again but, before he could speak, I was jogging to catch Laura, holding my belt buckle so my pants wouldn't fall down. I felt sour for letting David down, but then I caught the door, got into the fresh air, and the nastiness went away. I was ready for whatever.

If the movie started at 12:05, I should get to the bus stop around 1:45. The clock in Mama's car had said 11:47, so I had two hours. The spring air was thick with car engines humming. Laura was walking ahead with her left hand pancaked out over her head like it would keep her hair from frizzing up and going back.

"Hurry up, Kevin!"

Laura turned and walked backward, crinkling her nose and making the same tough face she'd made at Fingerwaves, then wiped her wet hand on her new black jacket and switched it with the right one. Saturday Night Laura in full effect.

Most days, I'd bust her down for yelling at me, but I didn't want her to ditch me, so I just said, "Sssmokin,'" real quiet and walked faster. I'd need to get some details about *The Mask* from David, in case Mama asked about it. Hope he's not too mad. Maybe he'd come to the mall next time, and we could start a special club where we rented all the movies we'd told Mama we were gonna see. Or maybe Aisha would change her mind, and we could watch it together, but we'd probably make out. I felt a little empty. No David for jokes, no Aisha for dates, just serious business with Laura.

I needed that day to be good if I was gonna risk getting put on punishment again. I just felt late to the world. All week, Demetric was going around fingering girls, that stupid Ace of Base song had hit number one, and David had beat Sonic 3. All I'd done was watch a thousand "Stop the Insanity" infomercials while the living room got shadowy before dinner.

Me and Laura stepped onto the little sidewalk by the mall's side entrance. I reached up my hoodie and scratched my back. Been itchy all week from the hair on my sheets.

"You gonna get scars if you keep poppin' zits," Laura said.

She was nice at home, but when we went somewhere, it was a whole 'nother story. You'd think I was a little baby, hugged up on her leg.

"What we gonna do, Laura?"

"I dunno. We'll see."

What if she went to the benches across from the food court and sent me off to kill time seeing what song they're playing at Chess King, or flipping through the rap tapes at Sam Goody while the manager with all the hair gel waited by the door to see if the alarm went off? It never does. I'm not a shoplifter. Laura couldn't send me off today, but why did she want me along?

I hoped David would see someone he knew and sit with them.

6
Paul

Paul walked to his car, rubbing his fingers against his palms so Sheila's lotion would seep in. Her lavender dish soap always dried his hands out. Its purple smell made crap appear in his mind because his pop would fill the bathroom with lavender air spray after he went to town on the toilet. Paul crinkled his nose. Pop would not be too pleased about this date, but Pop would appreciate how straight-up he'd been with Kevin. A good thing about people knowing was that Paul wouldn't have to worry what they would think. Instead, he knew the terrible things going through their minds. And when something goes through, it gets out. Having someone he cared about flip out made Paul feel even more alone. But things with Kevin would get better.

Rain dropped from Paul's hat brim when he unlocked the LeBaron. He bared his teeth in the rearview to check for bits of food and transferred his wet travel toothbrush from jacket pocket to glove compartment. It would be easier if he didn't care what Kevin thought. Paul had never thought of not telling as lying. It was protection, and protection didn't hurt people like lying.

What protected Xavier? He was open. That had caught Paul's eye right off. He was himself, not holding it in. But he wasn't exaggerated, with something to prove. He was natural.

Across the Lee Bridge, Xavier's mama's house was white with green trim. One of those little houses that made Paul think he could only stand upright under the roof's peak. Paul beeped twice, as instructed, and was glad he had his own place and didn't have to introduce dates to his folks. The black wood door opened, and Xavier took over the small porch, squinting in the rain as he turned to lock up, propping the iron storm door with his butt. He looked great. Hair in a wave on top, paisley rayon sport shirt and loose, light blue jeans that waved as he trotted across the short lawn. Paul clicked the button so Xavier could hear his automatic locks, then leaned across to open the door.

R&B station on, they headed to a breakfast spot downtown. Behind the wheel, Paul could keep his eyes on the road and pass off any silences to shifting gears and hitting signals.

"How many days off a week do you get?" Paul asked.

"Oh, two, but it depends which ones."

Xavier's right hand was cupped, rubbing across his left knuckles. "They pretty much always give me a weekend day, but sometimes I work both for the money."

Paul went "mmm-hmm" so hard they both laughed.

"How's the museum treating you?" Xavier asked.

"Like a baby treats a diaper."

Paul saw Xavier turn to him and trailed off. Didn't want to start fussing. Didn't want to put Xavier in work mode, making conversation he didn't give a damn about. Barbers and bartenders both get treated like shrinks.

Xaver said, "Well!" and both men laughed.

Paul said, "But what else is there? You like your job?"

"Well, you know, I'm just doing this until my singing career takes off."

Paul started rolling his eyes, but stopped at the rearview. No one behind them, bridge getting longer. Why did everyone think they were destined for stardom?

Xavier cranked the radio and rolled his tongue out of his mouth, screeching along to SWV, three keys off. Paul cringed and revved the gas in shock. "I don't really sing," Xavier deadpanned.

"No kiddin'," Paul laughed.

"Who do you know that don't hate their job, Paul?"

7

Kevin

We got in the mall and Laura took off, away from the food court. She was doing a new walk with quick, short steps and a bob to her shoulders. I caught up, heard her black Reeboks squeaking on the tiles, and asked, "What's up? Where to?"

"Oh, you'll see," she said, and raised her eyebrows. Mama would do the same thing, but her surprises were never that great. McDonald's for dinner. A trip to the pool where she'd prop her knobby feet up on a deck chair. Me and Laura were at the mall with twenty bucks and two hours to kill. We had a lot of choices. Lunch. Tapes. Maybe a hat.

She stopped at the racks of jewelry in the Claire's Boutique doorway. Everything in that store was pink and sparkling and making twinkly dance music. If I went in there, people would really think I was gay. What was Uncle Paul doing right then? Now, I'll always wonder if he's doing something gay when I'm not there.

"We are not going in there," I said.

Laura was already walking in. Come on, now! I looked at the leather store across the way and could

235

sorta smell the jackets. I wished my hoodie would turn into a black, zip-up leather like Uncle Paul's. Those jackets gay? I followed Laura, wondering what good this place could be. All the little earrings and necklaces shimmered and waved like jewels on a belly dancer.

This hard-looking white girl came out from behind the counter and said, "What's up, Laura," but it didn't sound like a question. She didn't look at me until Laura said, "Tracy, this my brother, Kevin."

Tracy said "Hi" in this fake voice that trailed off, like girls do when they see a baby. She had a long face with a pointy chin, a ponytail slicked back so hard her eyebrows popped up surprised, and so much makeup on her eyelids that they looked like my thumbnail after I whacked it with a hammer in woodshop. I nodded, "What's up."

"Is this on, or what?" Tracy asked Laura.

"Yeah."

Was what on? New tone of voice for Laura. Matched the fast new walk.

Tracy said, "I hear you wanna get your ear pierced, Kevin."

It sounded like Tracy was trying to crack on me. I did, though. Like crazy. To look like a rapper. Mama said I had to wait until I was eighteen, but I'd still ask every now and then, especially after seeing a bunch of high school guys with earrings.

"Yeah, I do," I said.

"Well, we can do that, but you're gonna owe me one."

When she said that, she touched my arm, right over the elbow. First Aisha, now her. Two girls touching my arm.

Owe her one? Did she want seven minutes of heaven in the employee lounge? All this time I spend looking at girls at school, wondering how to talk to them and how to get with them, and this might be how it gets started?

Who does she hang out with at her school? She didn't seem like a popular girl. If I got with her, would that make the popular girls like me less, or would it be good because I'd have some experience? Whatever. Making out with girls is making out, and I'm up for it.

Tracy touched my elbow, and I followed her over to a barber-looking chair on the far side of the counter. She didn't have a lot of booty under her jeans, but I watched it anyway. It's not every day a girl touches me, even a funny-looking, banana-face one like Tracy. I got a swell in my chest and felt my thing start chubbing up, so I slouched down in the chair and put my jacket in my lap.

Tracy gave me a fuzzy, black card with different earrings to pick. I got so excited that my throat got spitty and a tingle shot from my stomach to my butt.

I picked a small gold stud that maybe Mama wouldn't see if I kept her to my right and slept with my left ear down. Does Mama still check on me at night? I ain't a baby.

Tracy was jawing away at some watermelon gum while she stuck the earring in a blue plastic gun, then took a Sharpie and made a dot on my left earlobe. Her breath tickled my neck. I was glad David wasn't there because he'd be like, "Don't do it," then he'd do something gay like look at some necklaces. Tracy leaned in from behind, held up a hand mirror and asked, "How's that look?"

The face in the mirror was gray, mouth hanging open, because Tracy's hard little right tit was squished against my left shoulder. Aisha never did that! I pressed back. She took the mirror away and asked, "Well?" before I could look at the marker dot.

"It's good."

The jacket-in-the-lap had been a wise move. My scalp prickled. Had the movie started yet? Were there any good previews?

Tracy set the mirror on the counter and swung my chair to the left. Across the store, Laura held up some purple, dangly earrings and joked, "You gonna wear these, Kevin?"

I laughed, but kept my head still while Tracy put the earring gun on me. Sweat popped into my armpits, but somehow, I felt smooth in that chair, in that pink store. Would Uncle Paul come to a store like this? No. Uncle Paul was a man, even if he was gay. This gay stuff is confusing.

Laura walked out from behind a rack of necklaces and said, "You gonna cryyyyyy?" in the same baby voice. I felt like we were back at home on one of the good days, eating cans of vegetable beef soup with potato chips crushed into them.

"Alright, you ready, Kevin?" Tracy asked. I heard her squishing her gum up into her cheek.

"Yeah."

"One...Two...Three!"

There was a crunch that felt like popping a big zit. Laura clapped and did a little jump on the rug. Tracy handed me the mirror, and I saw the earring, like a golden egg in a fat purple bird's nest. Blood rushed to my ear, killing the hard-on. Thank goodness.

8

Laura dumped waffle fries on the wax paper from the chicken sandwich. She tore the end off a ketchup packet, and I covered the food with my hand and said, "No ketchup." Hate that stuff. She squeezed a little of it onto the back of my hand. I licked it off.

"Thought you hated ketchup, Kevin."

"I'm hungry though."

Laura poured the ketchup into the paper's corner.

I watched to make sure she didn't put any on the fries. The red blob made our lunch look like a painter's palette.

We were at one of the first food court tables. Laura kept looking over my shoulder to the high school kids hanging out at the fountain. I looked too. A couple boys sat on the backs of the benches, with their feet on the seats, and some girls, along with some other guys, stood around them, passing cigarettes and blowing thought bubbles of smoke over their heads.

My left ear was throbbing like the turn signal on a car. I asked, "You think Mama will see?"

"Well, I won't tell—Hey! Leave me some of that sandwich!"

I took another wolf bite before putting the sandwich back. There were pickles on it, too. I said no pickles.

Mama would notice anything, like that hickey under Laura's shirt last fall, but maybe she wouldn't look at my ear for at least a week. Then, I could wear the earring at school and see what Aisha said. And I could get some time before being on punishment again. And, by then, my damn ear would be done throbbing. Was it supposed to feel like this? Would Mama make me take it out? Better not.

"Speaking of not telling, I got you these," Laura said.

Laura tossed a white plastic card with a pair

of small gold hoop earrings onto the table next to the drink.

"When'd you do that?"

Since when did Laura steal?

"When you were busy having Tracy touch all up on you."

She flicked the earrings at me, then picked up the sandwich. My earlobe got hotter.

"Naw! She… What do you mean?"

I knew what she meant, but hoped she wouldn't answer. The last thing I wanted to do with my Saturday was talk about girls with my sister.

"I saw her getting all close with that earring gun."

Laura held her thumb and pointer finger in a gun and shimmied her shoulders, making a kissy face and doing a high-pitched girl voice, "Ooh Kevin, is this a alright place for me to put my *hole*?"

She balled up her gun hand, put it in front of her mouth, and laughed. I just stared, because I had to think about Laura having a "hole," Tracy having one, Laura noticing Tracy's hole, and if I'd missed something back at Claire's Boutique. Was I about to make out with Tracy? Is this how it goes down?

Sure didn't want Laura around if that was gonna happen. Me and Tracy in a shadowy corner by the drinking fountain, kissing with the front of my hoodie pulled up so our bodies pressed. Her soft stomach.

Her hard ribs and those handball-sized lumps. But every time I moved my head to avoid her nose, Laura was tapping my shoulder, going, "No, Kevin. Try it like this," then clamping my head between her hands to angle it just right. Nasty.

I wanted to know if Tracy liked me, but I didn't want to talk about it with Laura. Weird how a girl you wouldn't usually like was a lot cooler if she liked you. I looked at the little gold hoops dangling in my hand and asked, "When do I get to put one of these on?"

"Oh, you're going and changing the subject now."

"You want one of them? I only need one."

I held the earrings out, and Laura knocked my arm away, hard, so my sleeve squished into the big puddle of ketchup.

I shouted, "Dang!" then hopped up and hit my knee under the table. When I bent to grab my knee, I saw a old couple at the next table over pretending not to look. I tried to shake the ketchup paper off my hoodie. The earrings in my hand jangled, and I knocked over the soda. Hard as I was shaking, I expected the ketchup paper to fly across the mall to Thalheimer's, but it just turned over in the air and landed on my sneakers. Laura scooted her chair back, laughing at the river of orange soda pouring onto the floor. I balled up the paper and whipped it at her so it bounced off her face. Laura stopped laughing. I started. The cup rolled off the table and made a hollow pop on the floor tiles.

Laura stood up and said, "Let's go."

A guy with a mop was coming at our table, frowning. I stuffed the rest of the chicken sandwich in my mouth, and we hustled back to the side entrance, laughing and slapping each other's backs. The food caught in my throat, and when I looked at Laura, we started laughing all over again. I put my hand on her shoulder and bent, coughing while we busted out the door.

Back outside, the rain had stopped, but everything was dark and wet. Must have been more than a half hour into *The Mask*. I bet it started off with a bunch of funny stuff. Had Jim Carrey had turned into The Mask yet?

I could just see David in the theater, laughing and eating a big popcorn he got with money from his grandma. I'll ask him about it first thing tomorrow. How mad would he be at me? There was probably an empty seat next to David in the theater, where I should have been sitting. It would be cool to bust into the theater with my earring glittering in the line of light from the projector and sit next to David.

Laura grabbed my hoodie sleeve and wiped it off with a tissue from her clutch purse, saying, "Now remember, we went to the movies, right?"

After all this, Laura should have known we were

in it together. She wasn't the only one who was having a good time. I said, "I know. We'd both get in trouble, anyway."

"That's right," she said, handing me a tissue, too. "Getting grounded for calling Mama fat. The hell were you thinking, anyway?" Laura laughed. "Real gangster, Kevin."

I kneeled to wipe my shoes, but the tissue just turned to little white pills in the suede. Laura turned each side of her head toward her palm, patting down her hair. I wanted to say that standing up for myself didn't mean I was gangster, but Laura was already walking back into the mall. I followed her, getting excited and nervous as we headed toward the high school kids' benches.

Tracy was standing there with a lit cigarette in her mouth, tucking her pink Claire's nametag into the front pocket of her light jeans. She squinted at the smoke in her eyes, and there was something hot about her that I couldn't figure out. Not her face or body, but maybe how she moved, like she knew what was up. She sidled up to a light-skinned guy who might have been part Spanish and hugged him, nuzzling her nose on his shoulder.

He shrugged her off, then crammed his fists into his khaki jacket and stared over the heads of the people moving down the mall walkway. I felt a little sorry for Tracy, but that dude was cool. Let me shrug girls off sometime!

Tracy said, "That's my man," then saw us walking up and asked Laura, "Did you tell him about the plan?"

My earring throbbed. Plan? We gonna slip off somewhere? Would Part-Spanish care?

"Naw, not yet." Laura turned to me. "We need you to help us."

Help what? Lick the lunch out of Tracy's braces?

Tracy jumped in, voice plain and cold, "Remember how you owe me one? For the earring?" She nodded at my left ear. Throb. Part-Spanish was staring at Foot Locker, lighting a Black 'n' Mild.

"Yeah," I nodded and touched the bottom of my ear real light. Felt like it was full of hot water.

Tracy talked slow, bugging her eyes to make points. "Well, we wanna do some *shoppin'*, but we don't wanna be *bothered* while we're doin' it. That's where you come in. You got a girlfriend, Kevin?"

Oh snap!

"Uh, no. Not right now," I said. Maybe she did want to mess around. Laura smiled, and I snuck a peek at Part-Spanish. He was ignoring us.

"Well, let's say you did, and you needed to get her a gift," Tracy was still talking slow. "Could you talk to the clerk about that while me and Laura are, uh, *shoppin'*?"

Laura had a hand on her hip. Did Mama give her

extra money for clothes? No. Their type of shopping squeezed my throat, and I didn't want any part of it. Shoplifting is stupid. Who wants to get in trouble for taking things they don't need? But I owed Tracy one and didn't want to get my earring ripped out. Plus, last thing I wanted was to look like a baby. Maybe Tracy was about to dump that dude anyway.

"Yeah, alright. But I don't got any money." I was talking serious, heart whirring. I told Laura, "I need some money to flash. To say, 'I only got this much, and I wanna get a gift for my girlfriend.'"

If I was gonna do this, I'd do it right and not get caught. Besides, I wasn't stealing. Is it wrong to take clothes from a store with plenty to go around? Were some new clothes worth it? If I screwed up, Laura and Tracy might have to go to juvie. It would all be riding on me. The chicken sandwich started flipping on its bed of waffle fries, and I shut my eyes to settle it down. I wished that orange soda wasn't all over the food court floor.

What would Aisha think of this? Maybe she'd like me if I was a bad boy.

Inside my eyelids, I saw me, Laura, and Tracy in a gray jail cell with a cop pulling crying Mama away from the other side of the bars. When I opened my eyes, Tracy and Laura were waiting. Part-Spanish puffed his Black 'n' Mild. I couldn't make any excuses, so I made my voice hard and said, "Fine, let's do this."

9

My legs were pins and needles. I walked into the girls' clothing store, fingering the folded-up ten in my pocket. There was one clerk, and she was standing with Laura and Tracy by a shelf of designer jeans, smiling and sweeping her hands at Tracy's legs, then at the pants. Laura's hair was coming out the sides of her ponytail. She didn't look put-together like the clerk. That might have made Laura upset, but it set me at ease. We had plenty in common.

The clerk was a white girl, probably in college, with ringy hair and the tight, light-colored jeans that private school girls wear on weekends. She was also wearing a low-cut shirt, but I didn't look. I kept telling myself I was buying something for my girlfriend, and guys with girlfriends don't go around looking at other girls' chests. If I was with Aisha, I'd never get to look down girls' shirts. That would suck. Then again, I'd be able to look down Aisha's shirt as much as I pleased.

A couple minutes before, me, Laura, and Tracy had been sitting on a bench near the store.

"What are we doing?" I asked.

Neither of them said anything. Wanted to get this mess over with so I stood up and said, "Let's do this."

Laura put a hand on my thigh and said, "We

waitin' on the manager."

I sat back down. Tracy stared at the store and added, "That way, you can start asking the clerk questions like some dumb dude, and she'll leave us to do our business with those Guesses."

A grown woman with enough makeup for King Tut walked out, slapping a green and white cigarette box into her palm. Tracy said, "Aight."

I stopped near the counter, at a table with a "20% Off" sign. The earring got so hot that I worried it was leaking pus. I'd never even kissed a girl, and here I was in another girl store near all of these soft, small things that would go on their bodies. And I was about to help Laura and Tracy steal something. I'd never stolen anything in my life, unless that five from Tyrell counted. And that five made Tyrell want to fight me and David punch me, so what was gonna happen here?

I peeked up. Laura and Tracy had their backs to me, and hangers were clacking as the clerk shuffled through a rack of jeans. It was like looking at Demetric the day after he'd fingered that girl. They were new people, part of a whole world I wanted into so bad. My eyes got wet, and I looked through the blur at a dark green shirt on the table. One day, a girl's breasts would be filling up the smooth fabric in the front, right by my hands. The clerk walked up, smiling, and said, "Hi, how are you today?"

I was this close to yelling, "Horny! Scared! Not grounded anymore!" Instead, the words jumbled out, "I'mlookin'forsomethin'formygirlfrien'an'allIgotisten dollars."

The smile stayed on the clerk's face and she went, "Hmm?"

I held up the ten. My fingers were sweaty, making it soft. "All I got is this. And I need to get a present. For my girlfriend."

This time, I was too loud. I thought Laura was snickering across the store, but it might have just been the music. No matter what happened, we were supposed to pretend to not know each other, even if we look the same in the face.

The clerk came to life like I'd been winding a key in her back. "Well," she said, spreading her arms, "this is the Sale table. I bet we could find something here that she'd like. What size does she wear?" Crap. Size?

"D!"

She looked at me with one eye, then laughed a bit. "No, we do, like, Small, Medium, Large here. Is she about my size? Because I wear a Medium."

She unfolded a black shirt in front of her and said, "Would this fit on your girlfriend?"

My girlfriend. Just the idea of it. Wow. I met the clerk's eye and she smiled. In that second, I saw the powder over the bumps on her cheeks and how her right eyebrow ended narrower than the left one, and I liked her. Would those Guesses come out of her paycheck?

I leaned in on the shirt, pretending to be a rich guy inspecting a painting in a museum, and got lost in the black fabric until I couldn't tell how far it was from my face. I breathed in the cottony smell of new clothes, baby powder, and greasy food court lunch smells coming off the clerk. The shirt rippled and she said, "Excuse me, ladies?"

She sounded kinda fed up. Laura was in the entrance, stopped mid-step like she'd been sneaking through the night and heard a sound. Tracy was still heading out the door.

"What's under your jacket, Miss?" the clerk asked.

Tracy stopped and turned, insulted and frowning.

"My shirt. Whatchoo think?" said Tracy, in an even tougher voice.

The clerk said, "Unzip your jacket, please." Her voice wasn't warm at all anymore.

"What. You wanna check out my body?" Tracy rolled her neck out to the side.

The clerk said, "Miss..."

Laura looked at Tracy with her "Mama said..." expression.

I was in the wrong place, next to the clerk. I belonged with Laura, even Saturday Night Laura.

"…Do I need to call security?" asked the clerk.

Tracy stuck her chin forward and bunched her lips, then said, "Yeah," bobbing her head and squinting.

Still shielding herself with the black shirt, the clerk backed up and reached behind the counter for a cream-colored phone. Me and Laura's eyes locked. Her eyes were wide, and I could tell there was at least one pair of jeans under Tracy's jacket. I wanted her to read my mind and tell me if I should run, but she didn't. She just stood there, looking small, and I went back to when we were younger and both in trouble, waiting for Mama to figure out what to do with us. Then, Laura would say, "Well, it's done now. Ain't nothing we can do about it," and that would calm me down for some reason.

This had to be worse than "no TV for the weekend," though. When Demetric got caught taking some Now and Laters from the newsstand by Thalheimer's, he had to spend the next weekend sweeping up the mall floor, then he wasn't allowed back for a whole year. Now and Laters cost forty-five cents, Guess jeans cost at least forty-five bucks.

I slid my eyes away from Laura. Didn't want the clerk to catch on that we were together. Laura wouldn't say nothing, but would Tracy? Was I a sellout for not owning up to being with them? Why does staying out of trouble always make you a sellout?

The clerk was behind me, saying something

about a "pat-down" into the phone. Then she shouted, "Hey!"

Tracy was bolting out the store, bent at the waist with her left arm pressed to her chest and the right one flapping at her side. Two steps out, she kicked the wheel of a stroller, and the guy pushing it yanked it in close to himself and looked around, lips tight, all mad.

With the phone cradled in her ear, the clerk leaned out from behind the counter and watched Tracy go. "Yeah, toward the South Entrance," she said, shaking the black shirt at Tracy's back. "I'll be here with the other one."

The other *one*. I was free, but Laura sighed and plunked her butt down to the floor, hugging her knees toward her chest, looking at the white tiles around her.

A stumpy female security guard ran into the store, brought her chin in to give Laura a confused look, then ran at me with her left arm out and her right hand over the big flashlight on her belt. The clerk said, "No, her," and pointed at Laura.

Laura was still sitting. The security guard stood over her, blocking the door, and said, "Stand up, Miss."

Laura got up, eyes still on the floor. Her jacket hung open, and she was only wearing a tight white shirt under it. She wasn't hiding nothing.

The guard ran her hands under Laura's jacket, around her waistband and over her pockets, finding the clutch. She opened it, pulled out the hairbrush and peeked inside, then handed it back to Laura, who was still looking at the floor. The guard hopped out into the mall walkway to see if Tracy was still out there. So damn serious. Her and Mr. B would hit it off. She told the clerk, "Well, nothing here."

Tracy came back, stumbling because this smooth guard with a tight-clipped mustache was pushing the small of her back so she'd hurry. I'd seen him before, showing off his walky-talky to some high school girls. He was holding a pair of unfolded jeans in his other hand, with their legs flapping all limp and useless around his knee. They were the same light blue as the jeans that Tracy was already wearing. What was the point? Tracy was starting to seem like enough mess to cancel out the titty and earring.

For a second, all eyes were on the jeans. Then, Tracy looked at Laura, who shook her head, face crumpling as three tears streaked down her cheeks.

I wanted to creep out the door, but that would make everyone sure that I'd been part of this. Plus, if I walked past Laura and Tracy, they might say something and blow my cover. So, I stood stock still, like I'd do at school when Tyrell is messing with somebody and I don't wanna be seen watching.

I used my thumb to crunch the ten over my finger.

You wouldn't be stealing if you had money. Wished I had more. Then I could buy the jeans and act like it was a mistake. With the guards in the store, and the guy on his radio for back-up, the clerk turned back to me. "I'm so sorry about that, Sir. Do you like this shirt...for your girlfriend?"

It was balled up in her fist. She had no idea.

"Yeah," I said. "It's perfect."

"Wonderful."

We looked over at the guards and the girls. Tracy was staring into space on purpose, bopping her leg, with her opened jacket swinging a little. The female guard was between Tracy and Laura, so short that Laura had to hunch to show her her learner's permit.

I wanted to pull out my new earring, puke chicken fillet all over the soft shirts on the sale table, then run into the movie theater and hide under David's chair, carrying on about how sorry I was for ditching him. I wished it was two hours earlier and we were all in the car with Mama driving to a different movie theater.

The clerk went behind the counter and got out a red gift bag with black and white tissue paper. She rang up the shirt and folded it. The total was $9.44. That wouldn't leave me with enough for the bus. I'd have to walk home, but it would get me away from the security guards. Nevermind getting grounded all over again when I got back with a earring, a girl's shirt, and no Laura. I patted my pocket. I didn't even have my key.

I gave the clerk the ten. She gave me back two quarters, a nickel, and a penny. They fell into the corner of my jeans pocket and scraped my thigh while I walked out the store with my head turned away from my sister and that Tracy.

In the parking lot, the world was huge, the sky higher than any mall ceiling, and I just felt low. Laura was stuck inside, and I couldn't help. A car cruised by, looking for a spot in the full lot.

The clock over the camera store said 1:40. *The Mask* must have just been ending. If I found David, I could borrow a dollar, catch the bus, and act like Laura had ditched me. David could tell me about the movie while we rode back, in case Mama asked about it. I headed to the bus stop. The drizzle had started again, leaving blotches on the black paper in the gift bag. Maybe the shirt was Laura's size and she'd like it.

10

Paul

Tension broken, Paul and Xavier enjoyed breakfast. Paul even tried Xavier's Eggs Benedict, even though it looked like a pimple on a plate. The waiter was one of their people and didn't look at them funny. It was a new feeling for Paul, being out with Xavier and, well, being out. He felt like a movie character realizing he'd outrun his pursuer. The villain might pop back out in a minute, but for now, the world was a sigh of relief.

Paul wiped his mouth, placed the napkin in his lap, looked at his plate, and said, "X. I told my nephew about myself today."

Xavier paused with his knife cutting into the last bit of eggs.

"It didn't go too good."

Xavier shook his head and started moving the knife again. "What happened?"

"He'd been making a couple comments, and I was..." Paul brought his head up to speak over the brunch crowd's murmur. "I was tired of keeping secrets, you know?"

Xavier sat still, watching Paul while the restaurant bustled behind him, then said, "Secrets don't feel good."

Paul shook his head, picked up his napkin again, then dropped it in his lap. "No. He called me all sorts of things," both men gave pained half-smiles. "But, the worst was he called me a liar, for not telling him before."

Xavier swallowed his last bite. "This is that boy you brought into the shop last week?"

"Yeah."

"That's your homie right there. I can tell."

"Yeah."

"We all got uncles," Xavier said, nodding a bit,

and Paul remembered feeling excluded from the easy laughter when his Pop's brothers came by to watch the Redskins. "But they don't all take us to the barber on a Saturday. It might take him a minute, but he'll remember that."

The waiter dropped the check on the table, and Paul grabbed it. But when he reached into the pocket of his slacks, he got a mental image of his wallet on the back of his sister's toilet, where he'd left it while cleaning up.

"Thank you, Paul," Xavier was saying, fingers spread on the edge of the table.

"Actually, uh, X, I'm sorry. I—"

Xavier's eyebrow raised.

"—I left my wallet at my sister's. I … I wanted to pay and—"

"Don't worry." Xavier reached across the table and dashed two fingers across the back of Paul's hand before snatching the bill. "I did well yesterday. Fridays are always busy."

Xavier stared at the wall behind Paul's head, doing mental math, then managed to look dainty while lifting a buttcheek to reach for his wallet. And it made Paul feel worse.

"Thank you. Look, I wanted to take you out today. We gotta swing by there so I can get you back."

"I dunno. I like having the power here. What can I get you to do in return for breakfast?" Xavier tapped his pointer finger on his lips.

"Hey, we can do whatever, but I need my wallet."

11

Kevin

I stepped into the bus shelter. An old lady in a winter coat was sitting in the middle of the bench with shopping bags fanned out at her feet. I stood in the corner and watched the mall through the tinted glass. Soon, David would be walking up. Soon, I'd be on my way out of here. The old lady scooted down the bench and pulled her bags with her. Fine by me. I bounced the gift bag handles in the crook of my fingers and watched about twenty people getting bigger as they crossed the lot from the movie theater. Some broke away and went to the sidewalk that led to the bus stop. One of them had on a blue raincoat and walked like they needed to get where they were going. David.

As he got closer, I saw his hands pointing at ideas in the air. I was used to seeing him do that up close and having to duck back when he swung his hands too much. Who was he walking with? A girl. Still too far away to see much, but a girl for sure. Navy blue jacket and pink shoes. Little ball of ponytail bobbing up and down on top of her head. Glasses lenses silvery in the wet. A little taller than David. Not hard to be taller than David, but still, a girl.

Woulda known her if she was a girl from school. Had he met her before the movie and sat with her? I was supposed to do that today. Dang. Here I was, going crazy trying to get something done, and he just went to the movies and met a girl. And goddamn if he got any action before me, I don't know what I'd do.

David talking to the girl. Girl laughing, saying something back, pointing her ponytail back and forth. Old lady by me muttering some nonsense about the bus. Bag handles getting damp in my fingers. Dark green car rolling up to the corner of the lot by the sidewalk. The girl holding up a finger to the car, kinda waving, kinda saying, "Hold up." David stepping aside to let people pass and putting his hands in his raincoat pockets, real cool-like. Girl waving to David and getting in the car. David lifting a hand to wave back all casual, then turning to walk to the bus.

I leaned on the metal shelter post, watching him. The light rain made my forehead greasy. David looked through me, dropped his eyes to my shopping bag, and turned his head fast to check for the bus. When he finally walked up, I held up a hand for five and said, "D, how was the flick?"

He left me hanging and stared at my face, eyes narrow and snakey, head trembling. Some cars rolled up to the light by us.

"Why do you care how the movie was?" David

asked, forceful, from his gut.

A woman about Mama's age walked past, shaking her head at us, then turned into the shelter.

"I—"

"You leave me to sit alone in that movie like some kinda freak, and you still wanna know how it was?"

He spread his arms and leaned at me. I jumped, then felt stupid for being scared of David and his blue raincoat.

"I'm sorry, man. You wouldn't believe what happened while—"

"I wouldn't believe what happened?" David cocked his head. "I wouldn't believe that I'd been planning something with my best friend all week, and he ditches me at the last minute? Yeah. I wouldn't believe that. You right."

David started nodding and moving his head around like he was searching for something on the sidewalk. He sounded corny calling me his best friend, but it made me feel bad. He's my best friend, too. Kinda my only friend. He doesn't want to beat my ass, and he's always cool to kick it. That's more than I can say about anyone else.

"Dang," I said, scraping my shoe along the wet concrete. "Yo, I'm sorry…"

"And what's in that bag? Whatchoo been doing?"

"It's a shirt, 'cause—"

David shook his head. "A shirt. MF breaks plans

to buy a shirt."

I'd already apologized twice. What else could I do?

"David. What are you doing now?"

"I'm waiting for the bus so I can go home. Ain't you goin' home, too, or you got some other shopping to do?" David paused and eyed the bus shelter. "Where's your sister at?"

The old lady on the bench said, "Lower your voice, young man!"

I started thinking of something nasty to say about her ramen noodles-looking hair, but David beat me to it and said, "Lower deez nuts, you old bag."

What?! David wasn't much for cussing. Sometimes he still said "heck" instead of "hell." His voice was high-pitched, almost breaking, and I couldn't help but grin.

The old lady gathered her bags, then went to stand outside the other end of the shelter.

"Why are you laughing? You think I'm just around to be laughed at?"

"No. No. I just...Laura got caught stealing and I'm outta money and I don't know how I'm gonna get home and I was wondering if I could come to your place or something."

It sounded bad as I laid it out. As lousy as Laura getting caught and David being mad at me were, I hadn't realized just how terrible the whole day had been. Forget wishing I was still in the car with Mama, I wanted to rewind even further back and just be getting out of bed, enjoying that done-being-grounded feeling, and not cussing Uncle Paul. Jesus. Uncle Paul. Were we still gonna be cool?

"She got caught stealing?" David had an eyebrow up.

I said, "Yeah."

"Good!"

"What?"

"I said, 'Good!'"

"Why? That's my sister!"

I shoved David, and the shopping bag crumpled against his ribs. I was done feeling sorry and starting in on mad. Mad that David thought he could yell at me. Mad at David for getting some kind of girl action. Mad at Uncle Paul for being gay all this time and not saying nothing. Mad at Laura for getting caught. Mad I'd got into such a hole, and my friend wasn't going to help me out of it. David's butt rolled into the strip of mulch between the lot and the sidewalk, and his legs lifted before his heels thunked down into the dirt. His eyes got wild.

"I said, 'Good,' because that's what you get for messing around like that!" he yelled.

Did he think he was punishing me? Laura didn't need him acting like he could judge her. My left hand was swinging the shopping bag back and forth, and my right fist clenched, but as soon as I imagined knocking David's head into the dirt, he kept talking.

"Know what, though? Probably better you ditched me. If you'da been there, I never could have sat with Jaleesa. If you'da been there, you woulda scared her off. Acting like you the man…the man whose sister goes and gets arrested."

I turned away, then turned back. David stood up, and I pointed into his face and said, "That's my sister. You got no right to talk about her that way."

David came right back with, "Well, I'm your friend, and you got no right to treat me that way."

He said it quiet, digging his heels into the mulch. I got quiet, too, and I meant it when I said, "Then I guess we ain't friends."

I turned heel. The gift bag rose up, and I wanted to sidearm it into the street, but I held on. Needed to keep something from today. Couldn't have friends or an uncle, at least I could have this girl shirt. Walked to the corner of Broad St. with Laura and David and who the hell is Jaleesa in my head. Lots of pictures, but the only thing moving was me, walking alone down Broad St. Four miles? Three miles home? A long way in worn out sneakers. Maybe if the rain started up it'd clean the ketchup off my shoes.

I crossed to walk on the other side of Broad St. Maybe Mama would be driving by to get Laura from the cops at the mall, and she'd pick me up and be so glad I was OK that she wouldn't ask any questions.

Yeah right.

12

Couldn't tell you how long I was walking, but it felt like three years. And the longer it felt, the slower I walked, so the longer it took. I kept thinking about Laura, trying to decide if I should be mad at her for pulling me into that mess, or if that mess was a story that was gonna make me cool. Then I got scared she'd be in jail, and I'd be in trouble, and she'd think I was a sellout because I didn't get caught. That made me want to cry, so I stopped thinking about it and just saw the city at a crawl, looking in the windows of the car dealerships and doctor's offices I passed.

How do grown folks wind up working at these places? When kids get asked what they wanna be when they grow up, they all say, "A firefighter," or "President," or "David Robinson from the San Antonio Spurs." But there's only like two hundred guys in the NBA, and only one president, and he's white, and ain't but so much on fire. So, I guess other people have to sell cars and sit at the desk at a doctor's office telling people when to go in. Not what I want, though.

Mama must like babies, since she had me and Laura, but was she going through life telling people,

"When I grow up, I wanna work at a daycare in a church basement?" No. And I bet Uncle Paul didn't wake up one day in high school and want to be a security guard. Wouldn't be too bad to be like Uncle Paul and be in charge at a museum, but dang, Uncle Paul. A gay security guard?

Man, my legs were singing, hitting a high scream just under the back of my knees and sending a low burn across the front of my thighs. But it kinda felt good to be outside, doing what Mama calls, "Blowing off steam."

By the time I got on Overbrook Rd., my legs were numb, my fingers hurt from the shopping bag, and my right heel was stinging from where my sneaker had been rubbing. I stopped at the top of Battery Park, two blocks from home. The park's in-between some hills, and from where I was, I could look at the tops of the trees glistening green from the rain. There were some old guys who had spread newspaper to sit on the benches on the far end by Montrose. They all had cigarettes, and the smoke hung around their heads. On the tennis court, four teenage girls in tight jeans and puffy jackets stood around a stroller with a baby blue blanket. Some high school guys played a fast game of hoops, the ball slapping up and down the damp court.

The high school guys mess with middle school

guys who go to the park, but my feet hurt too much to go around, so I put my head down and walked in, trailing my fingers along the tall, black tennis court fence and watching grass swish against my shoes, looking down so no one would start with the, "What is you lookin' at?"

Came up on the basketball court, and the rhythm of the ball and sneakers got louder. Halfway there, on a mission. A shot rang off the backboard. Someone yelled, "Oh snap, Choo-Choo!"

Tyrell. Those weren't all high school guys playing basketball. Big middle school guys, too.

"Haha, damn," Leo said.

I cut right and sped up. Water flew from the grass as my toes kicked through it. Footsteps ran across the court and into the grass. I looked back and Tyrell and Leo, sweated up from playing ball, were coming after me like buffaloes in a Wild West painting. I took off running, and my right foot slipped in the grass while my left one twisted in some mud, then pushed off, getting halfway up the little hill by Montrose before Tyrell and Leo were on me. A wrecking ball fist smashed into my shoulder, and a big "Ohh!" came up from the guys on the court. Everything got too real. I stumbled and whipped around. On my right, Leo's lips were pursed like he tasted ball sweat. He crouched, expecting me to punch back. If I did, him and Tyrell would be on me, with their boys from the basketball court for back-up. If I didn't, I'd be a punk forever. I tossed the shopping bag behind me and puffed my chest, getting ready to send Leo spinning with a Mike Tyson uppercut. Don't mess with me. Then, Tyrell stepped up the hill, pointing and talking like someone's daddy, "Choo-Choo, you done too much this week."

Tyrell ain't my daddy, so I kicked him Bruce Lee style, but my leg was so tired, it just jammed into his thigh. One of the basketball guys hooted. Tyrell's eyes were dull like an animal's as he clamped a hand around my ankle and lifted my foot up and away from his gigantic, green basketball shorts. Leo snorted. My knee twisted as I fell and slid a few inches downhill, with Tyrell holding my foot and pulling my hamstring. Cats started laughing on the court. They wouldn't think it was so funny if they were in my place. I got so hyped that I felt sick and hated the whole world, even Laura. If she hadn't been playing at the mall, I wouldn't be here alone. Tyrell dropped my foot, and my heel sunk into the mud. Everything was getting dirty. I planted my hands to stand. Tyrell pointed at the torn up shopping bag and asked, "The hell is that?"

"Nothin'."

He kicked my upper arm, and the hurt matched my sore legs. Someone on the court yelled, "Yeah!" I fell again. Mud was clammy on the back of my head.

For half a second, I felt kinda relaxed, lying under Leo's huge shadow. Then, he grabbed the shopping bag from the hillside. Suddenly, I needed to gulp in air as fast as possible. But I couldn't. I had to keep cool and not let these MFs think they had me shook. I popped up so fast my stomach bounced, bending my knees for balance on the little hill.

From the corner of my eye, I saw Tyrell's fist growing bigger, then connecting with my jawbone, squishing into my left cheek and whirling me sideways. Back down, this time on my right arm with a tongue of mud tickling my ear. Shoulda had Aisha's tongue in my ear. I rolled onto my back, gulping air, and a blade of grass flapped off my lips. More laughing from the basketball court. A cigarette-scratchy voice yelled, "Get that nigga."

Tyrell stuck a nasty old sneaker on my chest, pushing out my breath, and asked Leo, "What he got?"

I tried to turn and look, but Tyrell jerked me with his foot. Leo was holding the bag open with both hands. He reminded me of a big, ugly Winnie the Pooh looking into a honey jar. "Some sorta shirt," he answered.

"Pssh," Tyrell said, taking his foot off my chest, grabbing my forearm, and hauling me to my feet. "Get up."

Leo dropped the bag on its side with the shirt

drooping out. I started to think, *Forget that shirt*, but then, *That's my shirt*. When I leaned to get it, Leo got me with a right that made his sides shake and pushed my gut sideways. I doubled over and saw the streak my heels had left in the ground. Tears. Dang. My throat quivered when I got my first slow breath, but the second time it didn't, and I knew it was time to get up to my full height and turn into a tornado of punches and spinkicks that would send Tyrell, Leo, and everyone on the basketball court flying. That idea stopped when Tyrell took a half step up the hill and pushed my shoulder to make me stand straight. Even from lower down the hill, Tyrell was blocking the little bit of sun. One side of his mouth curled up, then he said, "That shirt can't make up for sending me to the office," he paused and looked above me at the sky to tell God, "*twice* this week."

And it got serious all over again. Even more serious, because deep down, I knew I had it coming. If I ever got in that kind of trouble, I'd want to whoop whoever's fault it was, too, and Tyrell was the type of guy who made a habit out of whooping on people when he had less of a reason than that.

"But, we'll start with the shirt," he said.

I should have run right then, but I couldn't. I'd been dancing around all week, getting into it with this guy, and it had to come to an end. Leo grabbed my hood and twisted it around my neck, spinning my head and shoulders toward him. I pulled back, heard stitches ripping, and pictured myself having to wear that girl shirt home. Longest couple blocks ever. I let my body go forward, neck stuck to the side, and looked sideways at the guys watching on the basketball court with their eyebrows up and mouths open in dumb smiles. Then, Tyrell's sweaty, cigarettey smell hit me, worse than in PE, black oil in my nose. A punch pounded my kidney, and my legs gave out, so I was kneeling in the wet, hanging by my hood. A sneaker cracked into my tailbone and made me hop face-first into Leo's stomach. He went, "Oof!" and clamped both hands on the back of my head. My mouth filled with sweaty t-shirt. On Montrose, tires squealed, a door clicked open, then another, and footsteps clapped on the street.

Suddenly, Leo lost his grip, went "Oof!" again, then toppled onto me. I slid down the little hill, mud going up my shirt, with Leo's face in my buttcrack and his knee on the side of my head. The guys on the basketball court yelled, "Oh damn!"

All I could see was mud, but I heard, "Huh?"

A gay voice shouted, "Oh, hell no!"

One of the voices from the basketball court sounded confused. "There go that sissy from the barbershop."

Scuffling sounds. Feet ripping grass. Punches knocking air outta lungs. The same gay voice yelling,

"Get back on that court!"

Leo's knee pushed my face deeper into the mud as he rolled off me, and I was free. I stood. My back ached and my insides burned from the kidney punch. After I wiped the mud out my eyes, I saw Xavier the gay barber, face screwed up, pounding a left into Tyrell's stomach, then catching his face with a right uppercut when he buckled forward. Bam! Uncle Paul was standing next to Xavier and grabbed his shoulder saying, "Cool down, X. They just kids."

Tyrell's gut leapt as he stumbled backwards and fell at the bottom of the hill. Xavier watched with half a smile, then said, "I had to deal with kids like this not too long ago myself."

Uncle Paul was about to argue, but then Leo rushed them. Paul stepped forward and stopped him with an open hand to the chest. He looked awesome. His gold glasses were crooked, his turtleneck was half untucked, his shoulders were heaving, and the look on his face was a storm. He was a different man than the one who'd been sitting in the dining room that morning, riffing on Mama's cooking. That was ages ago.

Leo stepped back and said, "Hands off me, faggot."

For half a second, I was mad that Leo and Tyrell and all them would be able to crack about my uncle being gay, but then I got extra mad that he was calling

Uncle Paul a faggot. That's my uncle. Xavier yelled, "Oh no," and charged past Paul.

Two guys ran off the basketball court. The other two looked at their friends running, then at each other, realized they had to join in, and trotted along.

Xavier raised his fists and pounded Leo's shoulders, ears, neck, and head. His hands moved so fast he looked like a beetle on its back. Leo wobbled back, woozy.

I ran up to Uncle Paul, who turned with a fist cocked, then caught me in a hug and said, "My man."

Leo tripped on his own feet, then turned and belly-flopped at the bottom of the hill, six feet over from Tyrell, who was sitting up, mouth shiny red with blood. He tried to talk, but made a thick moan instead. The first guy from the basketball court stopped between them, did a double take, then said, "Oh. 'sup Paul?" and crouched down to check on Tyrell and Leo.

Uncle Paul squeezed me, then bounced me off his chest and out the way as the second guy from the basketball court punched him in the face and sent his gold glasses sparkling through the air. I caught my balance at the bottom of the hill in time to see Paul sprawling away and Xavier, with everything on his face in upside-down u-shapes, shoving the puncher over Tyrell and making him catch a few inches of air, back of his du-rag billowing, before sliding to a stop in the mud. On his hands and knees, booty pointing at the fight, Uncle Paul slapped the ground until he found his glasses, then stood and hung them from one ear. In a husky voice, he told Tyrell, "You best leave this boy alone unless you want more of that."

He turned and shouted at the guys from the basketball court, "Y'all heard?"

Xavier bucked, and fear brought Tyrell's face back to life. Then, Xavier threw a finger in the air and cocked out a hip, saying, "Think you all big trying to play like that." He shook his head. "Mmm-mmm. Two on one don't work."

It was crazy, because he looked gay as all get out while he was shouting at Tyrell and Leo, but the finger he was waving in the air was part of a fist that was starting to swell from whooping Tyrell, and his voice had a ragged, tough tone. One of the guys from the court laughed and punched his friend in the shoulder.

Uncle Paul shouted, "That's right," and rested a hand on Xavier's shoulder. When Xavier turned, Paul leaned in, swollen cheek and all, and planted a kiss on his mouth. Xavier's eyes grew wide, then drooped as he let his guard down and kissed Paul back for about a hundred years. Coughs and "Eww" noises rose up from the basketball guys, and Tyrell's head slumped back to the cool mud. I looked away, feeling rude for watching Uncle Paul kiss someone, jealous because I was supposed to be kissing someone that day, but nasty because Uncle Paul was kissing a dude. But at least he was kissing a badass dude who had just whooped Tyrell and could cut a ill fade.

Uncle Paul pulled his mouth away with a smacking noise and turned, licking his lips, to say, "And y'all saw that? If these two try and mess with anyone again, go 'head and spread the word that they got they asses kicked by a couple faggots."

The basketball guys went, "Oooh!" and a couple of them slapped daps. The guy who'd said, "'sup," to Uncle Paul looked like he'd heard a secret he wanted to tell. Uncle Paul put an arm around my shoulder, and for a second, I hoped it didn't make me look gay. Then, I decided I didn't care. Seeing a grown man punch someone from school wasn't right, but he did it to save me. He cares, and I can't say that about my pop. Me and Paul and Xavier walked back toward the LeBaron, which was still running on the street.

At the top of the hill, Uncle Paul picked up the shopping bag. One of the handles was hanging loose from a rip in the side.

"This yours, K?"

"Yeah."

Xavier eyed it with a brow up. I reached out for Paul to hand it over, but he said, "I dunno. This bag looks pretty gay to me."

Xavier nodded. Uncle Paul held it at arm's length, all suspicious, before pressing it into my chest and laughing out loud.

Uncle Paul said, "Get in the car, man."

He draped his arm back over my shoulders, and we walked to the LeBaron.

13
Paul

Paul's eyes popped to the rearview. Gray street rolling out behind the car, ten miles over the speed limit, putting more distance between him and the fight. Hadn't been in one of those in years. Maybe since he was those guys' age. What kind of man fights teenagers? One who's protecting his nephew. Wait, where the hell was Kevin?

"K?" he asked, voice raspy.

Kevin popped up in the backseat, horror movie-style, and said, "I was ducking down in case the police was coming."

Xavier, who'd been squeezing the seatbelt with both hands and glaring through the shotgun window, put a curled pointer finger over his lips to hide a smile. Paul said, "I think we good. We're real near your crib."

Kevin turned his head, slow and sly, to check out back. Xavier was palming down his hair in the side mirror.

"Don't get no mud on your uncle's car seats," he said.

Kevin snapped around and sat still. Paul coasted around the corner and onto Kevin's block of Hanes Ave., catching a whiff of Xavier's hair product. Smelled like the color orange. Like five kinds of fruit in a bowl under a palm tree. What would a vacation be like? He wanted to go on one, tomorrow.

He eased to a stop a couple doors up from the house and clicked the transmission into reverse. Late Saturday sun turning gold. Coming back from the park. All good things. Like a mini vacation, but after a fight with some teenagers. That wasn't right. The bite of Eggs Benedict bubbled in his stomach.

He belched under his breath, threw an elbow over the bench seat and nudged the LeBaron into a space. Kevin blocked half of the back window, sitting there with his brow knitted, conjuring something on the hood of the car. Inches from the turquoise Jeep Tracker behind them, Paul turned and cut the engine. Leaving the park, they'd sat for what felt like five years while Paul's shaking hands tried to jam his back door key into the ignition.

Kevin's lock clicked. Paul pressed the lock button and said, "Hold up."

Kevin tensed and glanced out the back window, "We gotta go in, before the police come."

"I don't think they're coming." Paul turned, and Kevin slid down in his seat. Paul continued, "What happened back there?" He paused and adjusted his glasses. "I don't want to ever do that again, even if it is for family."

The car was quiet without the engine on. At first, Kevin had been looking away from Paul and out the side window, but he'd turned back on "family."

"Now—"

Kevin cut him off. "Families ain't supposed to lie."

Xavier shifted in his seat and looked out the window, butting out as much as he could. Paul sighed. Kevin started to duck while a white sedan cruised by.

"You ever needed to keep something secret because you were scared what people would think?" Paul asked.

The boy's mouth was shut, but Paul knew he'd been there before. All teenagers had.

"That's kinda what it's like all the time for me."

Xavier picked at his cuticles. Kevin nodded and looked like he was about to say something. Paul wanted to wrap things up.

"We cool or what? I'm your uncle. It's not like I'm gonna try and make you my boyfriend."

Half a second pause in the car, then Xavier turned to Paul with an eyebrow up. Paul caught Kevin's eye, and the boy started to laugh. A real laugh that came out unexpected and hard.

In the space between the front headrests, Kevin and Paul hooked thumbs and did a soul five. As Kevin was leaning to the door, Paul said, "Wait. What was happening back there, anyway?"

Kevin puffed his chest and sunk into the seat. Xavier said, "Let's get inside. I'm not part of this family, but I'll still whoop somebody's ass."

EPILOGUE: NEXT MONDAY

Kevin

I'm on punishment through Friday. Mama said I deserved worse, but she was sick of having me around the house. Fine by me. Laura is in until the end of the school year, but I bet it'll get hot in May, she'll get fidgety on the couch, and Mama will let her go back out. I heard Laura laughing on the phone with Sharese last night.

After the fight at the park, Paul and Xavier brought me into the house. Soon as I smelled cooking and the stuff I can't describe that makes it smell like home and saw the rugs Mama vacuums, I felt worn out, beat-up, and dirty. Must have looked it, too, because Mama stopped on the third stair up, jingled her keys, and said, "Kevin, I thought—Paul? What are y'all doing here? Why you so dirty?"

The long answers to those two short questions popped into my head. Laura with the security guard. Tyrell's fist wobbling toward my face. All that time walking down Broad St. My eyes filled up and ran over.

Crying's no good anywhere, and it felt extra lame in front of Uncle Paul and Xavier after they'd won a fight for me. Then I wondered if they saw lots of dudes cry because they're gay. Probably not. Like, those gay dudes on *In Living Color* are a joke, and gay dudes don't always act like that. Xavier had proved that a few minutes ago. Shoot, Uncle Paul had been proving it this whole time. I just didn't know it.

Paul put his hand on my shoulder. Mama said, "I'm going to get Laura."

She caught my eye and said, "I guess you know." She had me, and there was no sense in trying to play it off.

"You're coming with me," she said. "But first, hurry up and go change."

I started upstairs and she said, "Wait, look at you. Those clothes are coming off. Right here," and pointed at the floor by Xavier's feet.

"Uh-uh," I said.

"Uh-uh what? Look at you!"

"I ain't takin' my clothes off in front of everybody!"

"It's just your uncle. He ain't gonna do—"

Then Xavier said, "Could I use your restroom?"

Mama pointed him up the stairs. He leaned on the door to pull off his shoes, then took each step one by one. I couldn't tell if he was walking all precise because he's gay or because his legs hurt from fighting.

"We need to get out of here, now. Train's leavin'," said Mama.

Paul kicked off his shoes and walked into the kitchen. I undid my belt. Paul came back, popping his wrists to open a trash bag, and said, "Put your muddy clothes in here. Toxic waste!"

I smiled, and wished Mama would, too. Her face was frozen in place. Stressed.

I wasn't too hot on running around upstairs in my boxers while Xavier was up there, so I hustled into my bedroom and shut the door before he was done in the bathroom. I got changed. Same t-shirt, different hoodie and jeans. Held the railing on the way down because every step made my back hurt, and I felt like an old man.

The stairs outside were hard, too. Mama stopped in front of the neighbor's house and said, "Come on!"

I was tired of people hustling me along, but I stepped it up and saw Mama walking faster, kinda bouncing. My thigh was tight every time my right foot hit the ground, but Mama was already at the car and didn't notice me limping.

We had to pass by the park on the way out

the neighborhood. The place where we had the fight should have had a plaque, like at Civil War battlefields, talking about my brave stand and how I got saved by reserves from another battalion. Instead, all I saw was a couple muddy streaks in the grass and life going on as usual. I didn't wanna say nothing, because I figured Mama was about this close to yelling, but when I looked over, it was even worse. She was leaning over the steering wheel, frowning at the road, and crying.

When I cry, Mama says something nice or hugs my shoulder. It makes me feel better, even when I'm crying because of something she said. We passed too close to a parked car, and I tried to decide just what Mama was crying about, then figured it was everything, so I said, "It'll be OK."

Would it, though? Was Laura gonna be in jail? Could she tell I'd been in a fight? Were Paul and Xavier gonna get it on in the house while we were gone? Naw.

Mama snuffled and lifted her glasses to wipe her cheek. Right when I thought she wasn't gonna say nothing, she went, "Will it?"

I wanted to say, "Yeah," and make her feel better. But I didn't know, and that was driving me crazy. Lotta things I don't know.

"I'm tired of this, Kevin."

Lord, here we go. Mama wiped at her eyes and

drifted into the middle of the street for a second.

"I'm the one trying to hold everything together, and I can't be there all the time, so I gotta know that y'all aren't gonna be acting some damn fools every time I leave you alone."

She was watching the road and blinking. We came to the stoplight at Chamberlayne and she turned to me. I ran my thumb under the seatbelt on my chest, wishing I was cruising past in a black Cherokee.

"I wanna come home to find the dishes done, not one of you locked up and the other one coming home looking like the creature from the Black Lagoon."

Mama was corny, talking about old movies. Then she said, "And what happened to you, anyway?"

Damn. Light changed, we started rolling.

"Me and Uncle Paul got in a fight."

Felt kinda proud.

"You what?"

I felt the car drifting and said, "Mama, look at the road."

"You got in a fight with your uncle?"

"No, like, I was in a fight with Tyrell," my head got hot and heavy, and I worked hard to keep the whine out of my voice, "and Uncle Paul and Xavier came and helped me."

Mama was dead quiet for a minute. A minute's a long time. Try holding your breath for that long. We passed the Virginia Union field with the old sign.

"Start at the beginning," she said,

"I was in a fight with Tyrell and Leo. In the park. And—"

"No, tell me everything that happened this afternoon."

She said, "everything," and my hand flew to my earring, then I moved it back to the seatbelt real quick. Everything? She didn't need to know that we didn't see the movie.

"We was at the mall—"

"*Were* at the mall."

"OK, OK. And Laura," I paused again, thinking how bad it would sound to say it out loud to Mama.

"Laura and this girl Tracy got caught taking a pair of jeans."

A black cloud came over the car, but I felt better. Since I'd said it, it wasn't just my problem anymore.

"Then what happened? Did the police come?"

"Security guards did."

We passed the boarded-up high school that Pop went to back in the day. I usually like to look at it and pretend the field next to it is mowed into a faded-green, old picture color, that the windows are shiny glass, and that a magic version of teenage Pop is about to walk out. Today, it just looked like a messed-up, old building.

"What did the security guards say?"

"I don't know."

"But you were there?"

Damn.

"Kevin?"

"I was there, but I wasn't stealing nothing. I was—"

"What is that in your ear?"

Paul

Xavier pointed Paul to Sheila's kitchen table. Paul was already sitting when he realized he was across from his usual spot. His lip was thick, and tasted of rusty, dried blood. His head was heavy with hot fluid. Xavier grabbed a handful of paper towels and turned to open the freezer. Paul looked at his ass and liked it. Not in a turn-around-on-the-street way, but in a satisfied way. This is good, this will do. The best things can be when nothing's wrong, not just when your mind is blown.

Xavier crossed the kitchen and lifted a nest of ice cubes and paper towels to Paul's face.

"You got some nerve, kissing me with a bloody lip like that," Xavier said.

Xavier's warm breath calmed Paul's forehead. "I'm sorry. I got caught in the moment."

Xavier dropped a hand to his shoulder and said, "So did Magic Johnson. Sure was a moment, though."

Paul laughed out his nose. The paper towels rustled.

"Look, X. I'll let you know for sure, I'm clean."

Xavier squeezed a tense spot in Paul's shoulder, and said, "Good, good. Me too."

Paul wrapped his right arm around the back of Xavier's thighs and hugged him, feeling at home in his sister's empty house. Next weekend, after the swelling went down, maybe they could go to DC and see Izola.

Kevin

Mama made me wait in the car, and she did that same fast-forward walk into the mall. The rain started up again, and I sat in the front seat, watching the drops race down the windshield and guessing which one would get to the bottom first. Was Laura in a dungeon under the mall? Would Mama come out alone, and we'd have to drive all the way to the police station?

A white lady parked next to the car, then jumped when she saw me sitting a couple feet away. I grilled her, but my mind flashed back to when Mama would leave Laura and me in the car while she got groceries, and we'd climb all around the backseat, making faces at people passing by.

How did Laura meet Tracy? Why did Laura decide

to take those jeans? It's messed up that she was cracking on me for trying to be gangsta earlier, but there she went, giving it a big try herself. Neither of us is really bad, but we got in a bad situation.

I leaned over to look at my earring in the rearview. Mama had just shook her head and went back to the road when she saw it. That was worse than if she'd yelled at me to take it out. The earring is proof that I'm bad, which is good at school and nothing but trouble at home. Tired of trouble. Wish Mama would chill. Then I'd chill, too.

The revolving door moved, and first Laura came out, then Mama. If they had some bags, I'd just think they'd been shopping and looked mad because they'd been fighting about what to get. Laura's shoulders were up with a hand over her head to stop the rain, and she was turned away from Mama. They both walked slow, like being in there had worn them out.

Man was I glad to see Laura, especially when she got closer, and I could tell that she didn't have a black eye or nothing from the cops. It was weird to see her still wearing her jeans with the little triangle of white shirt at the top of her jacket. Felt like days ago that I last saw her on the store floor.

Then the door opened and, for a second, I smelled wet air. Laura and Mama rustled in and clicked their seatbelts. I turned to Laura and said, "You got out!"

I thought I'd be joking, but I realized I'd meant it. It didn't matter, because neither of them said nothing. Mama just started the car, and did a fast u-turn to the parking lot exit.

I felt low for the rest of the weekend, like maybe the things I had before were great, and I'd just been too worked up trying to get the next thing to really see it. I was a little late to the bus this morning and had to run for it. When I saw David, I cheered up and started thinking about the laughing we hadn't done since Saturday. I sat in the seat behind him and said, "Sssmokin'!" just loud enough for him to hear. He sat still, bouncing with the bus for a second 'til I was about to say it louder, then he turned around and said, "Yeah?" And I thought about how people who say "Sorry" all the time are wack because they need to figure out how to not get in those situations in the first place, but people who say "Sorry" every now and then have a good reason. So, I said, "Yo, I'm sorry about Saturday, D," and put my hand up for five.

He didn't make it easy, though. He left me hanging, put a hand on the back of his seat, and said, "You just sayin' that 'cos Laura got arrested."

Janelle looked over at us, listening in. I ignored her and leaned in. "Not arrested. They just took her to some security room in the mall."

He started to turn back, so I said, "And I'd be sorry for running off whether or not she'd got in trouble."

I wanted to say I'd been thinking of him the whole time at the mall, but that sounded kinda weird. It's not easy to tell people, especially other dudes, that you care about them. Before, I woulda said it sounded gay, but I'm trying not to trip about that anymore. Seeing Xavier go off on Tyrell and Leo gave me some new ideas about what being gay is. It also made me think about how grown folks still have to deal with some of the same mess that we do, so there's no sense in rushing to get grown.

Janelle's eyes were still on me. David ducked his head down behind the seat. I wanted to take back all the nice things I said, because I knew he was about to tell me off. Then, he popped back up, wiggled his shoulders back and forth, and yelled, "Ssssmokin'!"

The bus driver looked back in the big mirror over the windshield and shouted, "Face forward in your seat, boy!"

David sat down, and I went up an aisle to join him. Bad as I was at being his friend, I was even worse at not being it.

The stretch of hall by Aisha's locker was warm when I walked through before last period. I watched the sunbeams so I wouldn't have to look at her locker and remember how good she felt hugging me. And guess what I saw? Demetric from behind, with a tuft of orange hair over his left shoulder and arms with white Adidas stripes on them crossed on his back. My foot skidded. For half a second, I forgot how to walk. Then, I picked up the pace and kept peeking while my face got hot. As I passed, I slid my eyes to the side and saw Aisha's puffy cheek pushed into the chest of Demetric's green and navy Hilfiger jacket. She saw me and started to open her mouth, but I turned my head and sped up. My heart felt huge, and I thought I was gonna puke or crap it out, or both. Behind me, I heard him go, "What?" in a just-woke-up voice. Their jackets rustled together.

I should have known something was up with them. I probably did. But, I dunno. I wanted her but didn't need her. And, I'd forgotten all about her when that nasty Tracy was touching on me on Saturday, so I knew she wouldn't be in my head forever. But, know what else isn't forever? People going out. Maybe she'd go out with me after Demetric. And maybe I'd be with a different chick by then, a chick who doesn't like corny-joke dudes like Demetric.

This girl Shanelle who sits behind me in English had smiled and asked, "You get your ear pierced, Kevin?" and I said, "Yeah," and smiled back. She's one of those chicks you don't notice is pretty until you really look. When Mama told me to "Keep the damn earring" so I could think about what I did every time

I saw it, I doubt she meant like that, but whatever. If my time isn't now, it feels like it's about to be, like I'm a rock on the edge of a cliff, about to roll down, making out with lots of girls.

Me and David were walking back from the bus. It was super nice out. Wasn't hyped on being on punishment again, but wasn't much I could do but ride it out.

"Tameka just had to say something, huh?" I said.

I'd tried to creep by the project girls in lunch, but Tameka must have smelled me, because she turned around and went, "Why you was lyin' about goin' out with that trick?"

I don't think Aisha's a trick, but I am kinda salty about her canceling our date. And, I sure hadn't been lying, but no way to prove that. I got crossed up, holding my lunch tray with David behind me. Then, I was like, *How would Eddie Murphy handle this one?* and it hit me, Tameka is nothing! I cheesed like Eddie Murphy and said, "Hush it. No one cares what you think," and strutted off, bag of tater tots sliding across my tray. I was in my seat before Tameka's friends quieted down from going, "Ooooh," so she could say something back.

I walked slow, kicking a soda can on the sidewalk and said, "Yeah. But I ain't trying to listen," and David nodded.

Tyrell came around the corner, and David started

looking for grown folks or escape routes or tree branches he could use as weapons. But, I just glared, and Tyrell shrunk into himself, like his whole body was folding into the crease on top of his gut, man-boobs and all.

David stepped onto the grass, starting to cross the street, but I swatted his elbow and said, "It's cool."

"Huh?"

"Just keep walking. We cool."

Tyrell was thirty feet away, watching the sidewalk. His lower lip looked like a funnel cake. I held my head high. Tyrell stepped out and walked through the grass between the sidewalk and the street. I said, "Wassup."

Tyrell whispered, "Wassup," back and kept walking, faster.

David looked at me like, *What?*

I shrugged. "We cool now."

"We are?"

"Yeah. We all are."

Even if I was trying to take back ditching David, there were some things I'm glad had happened on Saturday. Speaking of, remember Jaleesa who he sat with at the movies? That's his cousin. I found out when I asked if he was gonna get with her. Nasty. So, I could still be the first of us to get a girl.

The sun was to my back, warming my head. My shadow stretched out along the sidewalk, and I ran my hand up the hair growing in soft from my fade. Uncle Paul said he'd take me back to Xavier's shop, and I couldn't wait.

THANK YOU

The Columbia College Chicago Fiction Writing Department, for taking a risk on a brother with a C average.

My thesis advisor Don De Grazia, Audrey Niffenegger's Spring 2012 Big Books class, Alexis Pride's Fall 2010 Thesis Development class, Laurie Lawlor's Spring 2009 Young Adult Fiction class (May Robertson!), Eric May, and Donell Bonaparte.

Jacob S. Knabb for bringing me into the fold at Curbside Splendor. Victor David Giron for runnin' thangs, and Leonard Vance for editing them.

Chicago Reader, Curbside Splendor, Great Lakes Review, Hair Trigger, and *Trilling Magazine*, for publishing excerpts of this novel.

Everyone who wrote a blurb, especially Adam Mansbach, for the inspiration, extra time, support, and advice.

My wife, Sharon A. Mooney.

Richmond, VA 23222

Born to an African-American father and an Irish-American mother, Chris L. Terry spent his teens and early twenties touring the world in a punk band. He has a Fiction Writing MFA from Columbia College Chicago, where he now works in Student Engagement. *Zero Fade* is his first novel. For more of his writing, visit ChrisLTerry.com.

CURBSIDE SPLENDOR

www.curbsidesplendor.com